"What have you got against romance, Chapel? Against me?" Ben asked.

"Why—"

He went on before she could answer. "You're a beautiful, desirable woman, you know, and standing there in that satin robe, you fill my head with thoughts of loving you this instant!"

Chapel was stunned for a moment, then answered his challenge. "Ben, you don't know what you're saying! You don't even know me!"

"I know you want my column banned because I advocate romantic behavior between men and women—that tells me an awful lot! I mean, sometimes a man and woman want to do more than just—talk," he finished.

"Oh, would you get out of my house now, before I throw something?"

"There's a blizzard out there!"

"Tough tootsies!"

"I'm not going!" he insisted.

"I'll call the police!" she threatened.

"Can't. The lines are down. So I'm staying. Now, go and put some clothes on before I lose control and ravish that delectable body!"

"Ravish my body?" A bubble of laughter escaped her lips. "I thought only pirates did that. This is getting good!"

Ben shook his head, laughing softly. "You are really something, Chapel. One minute you're shouting from the barricades, and the next you fill the room with sunshiny laughter. You're hard to keep track of."

Chapel only smiled. . . .

WHAT ARE *LOVESWEPT* ROMANCES?

They are stories of true romance and touching emotion. We believe those two very important ingredients are constants in our highly sensual and very believable stories in the *LOVESWEPT* line. Our goal is to give you, the reader, stories of consistently high quality that may sometimes make you laugh, sometimes make you cry, but are always fresh and creative and contain many delightful surprises within their pages.

Most romance fans read an enormous number of books. Those they truly love, they keep. Others may be traded with friends and soon forgotten. We hope that each *LOVESWEPT* romance will be a treasure—a "keeper." We will always try to publish

LOVE STORIES YOU'LL NEVER FORGET
BY AUTHORS YOU'LL ALWAYS REMEMBER

The Editors

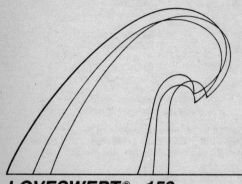

LOVESWEPT® • 153

Joan Elliott Pickart
Mister Lonelyhearts

 BANTAM BOOKS
TORONTO • NEW YORK • LONDON • SYDNEY • AUCKLAND

MISTER LONELYHEARTS

A Bantam Book / August 1986

Cover artwork by Walter Popp.

ISBN 0-553-21770-4

Published simultaneously in the United States and Canada

---

*Bantam Books are published by Bantam Books, Inc.
Its trademark, consisting of the words "Bantam Books"
and the portrayal of a rooster, is Registered in U.S. Patent
and Trademark Office and in other countries. Marca
Registrada. Bantam Books, Inc., 666 Fifth Avenue, New York,
New York 10103.*

PRINTED IN THE UNITED STATES OF AMERICA

O   0 9 8 7 6 5 4 3 2 1

For the three *P*'s—
Pat Elliott Hunt,
Patty Alexander,
Patti Herwick.

Thank you, dear friends.

One

Ben Simmons was bored.

No, he mused, that wasn't the word he wanted. It wasn't boredom, but more of an inner restlessness, a vague sense of dissatisfaction. It had been plaguing him for weeks now, but he couldn't put his finger on the source of his discontentment. Midlife crisis? he wondered. At thirty-five? No, it was something else. He wished to hell he could figure it out, so he could fix it and move on with his life.

Ben braced his hands on each side of the window-frame and stared out at the thickly falling snow. Detroit was being transformed into a marshmallow fairyland, and six floors below the traffic was moving at a crawl. When he'd entered the building, he'd seen a red-suited Santa Claus standing on the corner ringing a bell, and he'd wondered absently if the guy was frozen stiff.

Ben's thoughts skittered to his home in Santa Fe, New Mexico. When he'd left there yesterday the sky was clear and blue, the sun a golden globe warming the desert. He'd grabbed a quick lunch of homemade tamales from one of the vendors lining the street adjacent to the Palace of the Governors before dashing to the airport to catch his plane. And he hadn't flirted with any of the female flight attendants during the trip, which was another glaring bit of evidence that he was off-kilter.

"Damn," he muttered, scowling. What was wrong with him? His life had undergone fantastic, unbelievable changes in the past year. He'd advanced as far as possible in his job as a reporter for the *Santa Fe Sun* and had been seriously considering applying for a position on a larger newspaper when he had suddenly been catapulted to a nationally known syndicated columnist. His "Dear Ben" advise column had taken off in popularity like a rocket, and he was a household word.

He had money, prestige, women flocking after him. He'd been on magazine covers, interviewed by Donahue, and had traveled across the country to appear on talk shows like this one in Detroit. He had it all. He had it made. Yet he was edgy as hell. It was as though he were seeking something that was just around the corner, but he couldn't find the damn corner!

Maybe he should have talked to Austin about this

when she was in Santa Fe last week. But she'd been so involved in the arrangements for the christening of her and Patrick's baby boy that Ben had hardly had a chance to see her before they'd flown back to Paris. Austin had been glowing with happiness, and Patrick had seemed never to take his eyes off her and their son. That was nice, Ben thought, really nice. Austin deserved the best. They'd had some good times together when she was a reporter for the *Sun*. She was the only one who'd gotten away with calling him Benny. At first she'd been frightened at the prospect of leaving her safe little world and marrying wealthy Patrick Moran, who owned the paper along with a multitude of other businesses, but she and Patrick were doing great, and Ben was happy for her.

It had, in fact, been Austin's marrying Patrick that had changed Ben's life. Austin had written the "Dear Auntie Rose" advice column for the *Sun*, and Cappy, the editor in chief, had dumped the project into Ben's lap when Austin left. Ben had taken it over as a lark, and the response had been overwhelming! The public had been intrigued with the idea of a man's giving advice to the lovelorn, and the mail had flooded in. Three months later Patrick was approached by a major syndicate, and now the column was printed daily in over fifty major cities across the United States.

Yes, it had been quite a year, and Ben was grateful. He felt guilty for having this new sense of emptiness, the ongoing restlessness. He had made it to the big time and should sit back and enjoy it, Ben told himself. His agent said the offers for speaking engagements, more television shows, and interviews for slick magazines were pouring in. Fan clubs for Ben were springing up across the country, and Cappy had hired a secretary to take care of Ben's mail.

And right smack-dab in the middle of his life was this void, and it was driving him nuts!

"Mr. Simmons," a woman behind him suddenly said. "I need to check your makeup."

"Sure," he said, turning to face her. "Turn me into something gorgeous."

"You look pretty good to me right now," she said, watching as he settled into a chair. "You'll make the others appear half dead because of that tan."

Ben studied his reflection in the mirror as the woman draped a plastic sheet around his broad shoulders. He was deeply tanned from jogging and swimming in Santa Fe. His hair was strange, all different shades—from light blond to medium brown. Sexy, the women called it. They also said his eyes were like fudge sauce, chocolate chips, a teddy bear's. One woman even said he had bedroom eyes. He knew he was good-looking and kept himself in shape, but why were women fawning over him now? he asked himself. He didn't look *that* great!

"You don't really need anything except a bit of powder to tone down your healthy glow," the woman said. "Mrs. Emerson will be in to— Oh, here she is."

A stout woman in her fifties bustled in the door with a clipboard in her hand and two pencils stuck haphazardly in her hair.

"Mr. Simmons," she boomed, "how absolutely marvelous to have you with us on *Opposite Views* today. I trust your hotel suite is comfortable? The limo arrived on time? You have everything you need?"

"Yes, I—"

"Splendid. Now, I just want to cover a few things with you. Our show is syndicated and will be taped. Any real bloopers will be cut, so don't worry about that. We have a live audience and we take call-in questions. There's a seven-second delay on the calls to screen the sickos. Hopefully. The host, John Swanson, knows his business."

"I'm sure he does," Ben said, getting to his feet as the plastic sheet was whisked away. "I understand my opponent is a woman lawyer."

"Not opponent, Mr. Simmons," Mrs. Emerson said. "Simply someone with an opposite view from yours, which is the crux of our show: to present two sides to every coin. Dr. Barclay has gained quite a reputation in Detroit for supporting the cause of women. She takes endless cases of sex discrimination, abuse, unpaid child support, what have you."

"A dyed-in-the-wool feminist," Ben said, smiling. "Ten bucks says she hates men."

"I adore men," the makeup woman said, as she left the room. "Absolutely adore the creatures."

Ben chuckled softly. "So okay, Doc Barclay doesn't approve of my column, right?"

"Right," Mrs. Emerson said. "She feels it's demeaning to both men and women because you advocate the extensive use of romance in a relationship. Poppycock, I say to her opinion. You should have seen my Arthur's face the night I met him at the door in my black negligee, the way you recommended in your column. Arthur didn't vegetate in front of the television *that* night, I'll tell you! I'm going to do the bit about renting time in a private hot tub next. Ought to curl his toes."

"Good for you," Ben said. "Put a little zip back into your marriage. I assume Arthur has come through with some romantic interludes of his own making?"

"You'd better believe it! Well, you're on in a few minutes. Someone will come for you. It was a pleasure meeting you. I'm one of your biggest fans, and Arthur definitely is too. I didn't realize he was still so . . . healthy. Goodness! Ta-ta."

"Bye," Ben said, smiling as she left the room. So Dr. Barclay was a cold fish, he mused. She probably looked like a fullback for the Detroit Lions. He knew the type. They yelled for equal rights, and would deck any guy who tried to open a door for them. Those gals no doubt thought a hot tub was a place to do their laundry! Oh, well, at least this show would be different from the others he'd done, where he'd just given out advice to the audience and people calling in. The hour might be halfway interesting.

Ben shrugged into his tan jacket and adjusted his brown tie over his pale shirt. The suit was custom-made and fit him perfectly, which was another new element in his life after his meager wages at the *Sun*. Lots of classy changes had taken place, all right. He even went to a hair stylist now, instead of a barber. That was too bad. His barber used to know some great dirty jokes. So bring on rough, tough, mean old Dr. Barclay, he thought. He was ready!

Chapel Barclay smoothed her auburn hair back from her temples yet another time, then adjusted her gray wool skirt over her slim hips. Further fussing brought a tug on the gray blazer, and a straightening of the collar of her pale yellow silk blouse.

She did not, she reaffirmed in her mind, want to go on television! Those weren't butterflies in her stomach, they were eagles. This whole thing was ridiculous, ludicrous, asinine! She didn't belong on television. Her place was in the courtroom, where she presented herself with dignity, intelligence, and a determination to succeed. She was respected by her peers—even feared by a few—for her fierce attacks on the perpetrators of justice.

Yet here she was about to appear on the boob tube with the most infuriating male chauvinist on the face of the earth. Ben Simmons. "Dear Ben." Blak! She detested the man, although she'd never met him. His advice column was an insult to women. He advocated the use of feminine wiles to snare, and hold on to, a man. Sex and silk were the key, said the great Mr. Simmons. Flaunt your body, wiggle your tush, show some thigh, and bingo! The guy was yours. Sick!

And Ben Simmons's advice to men was just as bad. According to "Dear Ben," men should revert to the customs of the Victorian era with offerings of flowers and candy, nonsensical gifts of little meaning to express so-called romantic messages. Dim the lights, turn on soft music, massage her feet. Good grief! What had happened to communication, to two people talking to each other, sharing their minds and not just their bodies?

She'd seen Ben Simmons's picture on the front of magazines. He always looked so darn smug, as though—if it weren't for him—there'd be no loving couples left in the entire country. Granted, he was good-looking, but that didn't give him the right to dictate his whims to the populace!

Chapel had read his column every morning for months, and grown angrier by the day. When he'd advised a woman to deck herself out in a red bow and give herself to her lover as a birthday present, that had capped it. A red bow, for Pete's sake. Just bare flesh and a big red bow!

The letter Chapel had written to the editor of *The Detroit Star* had been short and to the point. Ben Simmons was setting both men and women back decades in their quest to be treated as equals capable of functioning from the neck up as well as down. The woman of today had brains as well as breasts, the men had more than muscles, and it was time Mr. Simmons recognized that fact. He was a menace and his column should be banned!

It was amazing, Chapel thought, frowning at the ceiling, what a tiny letter could do. The paper had been deluged with responses—some pro, some con—after her tirade had been published. Then three weeks later the program director of *Opposite Views* had called to ask her to appear on the show with Ben Simmons. She'd been so stunned, she said yes without thinking, and now here she was, about to go on television with a man she'd rather strangle with her bare hands!

"Dr. Barclay?" a young man said, poking his head in the door. "All set?"

"No!" she said. "I mean, yes, of course, I am. Certainly. Fine." Oh, super! Now she was babbling!

Chapel touched the chignon at the nape of her

neck, then lifted her chin determinedly and marched from the room.

"Dear me," Mrs. Emerson said, hurrying into the room and startling Ben, "I'm not my usual efficient self today. I was supposed to have you read Dr. Barclay's letter to the editor before you went on the air. Here." She shoved a newspaper into his hands.

Ben scanned Dr. Barclay's letter quickly, his eyes widening as he whooped with laughter.

"I should recognize the fact that 'women have brains as well as breasts, men have more than muscles'?" he said. "I love it! Doc Barclay has a real flair with words. She wants my column banned? Oh, good Lord." He laughed again. "I can't believe this!"

"Ready, Mr. Simmons?" a man asked from the doorway.

"You bet I am," Ben said, smiling broadly. "I have a feeling this is going to be very, very interesting. And definitely not boring!"

Ben was led down a corridor to the edge of the television stage set. He could see a typical talk-show grouping of low table and plush chairs. The chatter of the audience reached his ears.

"Ben Simmons?" a man said, extending his hand. "I'm John Swanson, the host of *Opposite Views*."

"Pleased to meet you," Ben said, shaking hands.

John Swanson was a handsome man in his forties, impeccably dressed in a three-piece suit, and flashing a toothpaste-commercial smile. He looked the part of a talk-show host, Ben decided, complete with capped teeth and a suspiciously phony-looking clump of hair at the back of his head that no doubt covered a bald spot. So where was the discus thrower, old Doc Barclay?

"Ahh," John said, beaming from ear to ear, "here is our other guest, whom I've had the pleasure of meeting already. Dr. Chapel Barclay, may I present Mr. Ben Simmons."

Ben turned, and in the next instant felt as though he had been punched in the stomach. He was staring down into the greenest eyes he had ever seen. He blinked once slowly, then noticed that the eyes were set in a face with delicate features and smooth ivory skin. Hair the color of cinnamon was pulled tightly back, and he wondered how long that hair was, and how it would look hanging free. Her figure was camouflaged by an ultraconservative suit and prim blouse, but her full breasts could not be completely concealed. She was maybe five feet five without the high heels, and she was lovely! Dr. Chapel Barclay was a beautiful woman!

"Dr. Barclay," he said, extending his hand to her.

The magazines hadn't done Ben Simmons justice, Chapel thought wildly, slowly lifting her hand to place it in his. He was taller than she'd realized, probably at least six feet tall, his shoulders were wider, and his eyes— Oh, dear heaven, those eyes! They were dark and fathomless. His hair was so thick, all different shades from blond to brown. Ben Simmons was . . . was Ben Simmons! A chauvinist! A nerd!

"Mr. Simmons," she said, nodding slightly, as she retrieved her hand. No, she thought firmly, the heat from his hand had not warmed her entire body. Don't be silly. She had to get a grip on herself. This whole television nonsense had really jangled her nerves.

"Now, then," John Swanson said, "a few ground rules. No foul language. Let's keep it clean. The camera will open with both of you on stage; I'll give a brief sketch of who you are, then ask for your stand on the issue. Mr. Simmons—Ben—you'll explain why you write the "Dear Ben" column, then Dr. Barclay, you can express your objections to it, or I may do it in reverse order. We go to audience questions, then call-ins. It's all taped, we edit it later, and it will be aired tomorrow morning. Any questions?" They both shook their heads. "Okay, let's go on the set."

"Dr. Barclay?" Ben said, stepping back with a sweep of his arm and smiling at her.

"Thank you," she said tightly, moving past him. What a smile! she thought. It just lit up that gorgeous, tanned face, and his eyes sparkled. They did! They sparkled. Oh, super. Her nerves were so shot, she was getting hysterical. She didn't give a diddly about Ben Simmons's smile.

A roar of applause went up from the audience as the trio walked on stage. John Swanson smiled and waved, then motioned Chapel and Ben into the chairs, with Chapel in the middle, and sat down himself. A member of the crew affixed mikes on each of them.

"Thirty seconds," a man yelled, then held up a card in front of the audience that cued an increase of applause.

Nice, Ben thought, as Chapel crossed her legs, then tugged at her skirt. She wasn't very big; in fact, she was sort of fragile-looking. He could probably span her waist with his hands. She also looked mad as hell. Well, what did he expect from a woman who wanted him banned!

"Five seconds," the man said. "Four . . . three . . . two . . . You're on!"

"Ladies and gentlemen!" a voice boomed, causing Chapel to jump. "It's time for your favorite talk show . . . originating from Detroit . . . *Opposite Views*! Write down the number you see on your screen so you can call in your questions to our guests. And now, let's say good morning to your host, John Swanson!"

"Good morning and thank you," John said to the cheering audience and the red light on the camera. "Our guests today are Dr. Chapel Barclay, a prominent Detroit attorney, and Mr. Ben Simmons, who writes the syndicated advice column 'Dear Ben.' Please give them a warm welcome."

The audience applauded enthusiastically as the camera swept over Chapel and Ben. Ben smiled engagingly. Chapel stared at the machine with wide eyes, as she clutched her hands tightly in her lap.

She's scared to death, Ben thought suddenly. She looked as if she were going to faint dead on the floor!

"Relax," he whispered, as the camera panned back to John. "Pretend you're home in your own living room."

"Easy for you to say," she mumbled, not looking at him. "I've never done this before."

"You'll be fine. Trust me."

"Ha!"

Ben chuckled softly and settled back in his chair. In the next instant his attention was riveted on John Swanson as the host explained that, in addition to being an attorney, Chapel Barclay had a doctorate in economics. She had voiced adamant disapproval over the "Dear Ben" column in the form of her letter to the editor of *The Detroit Star*.

She was a smart woman, Ben thought. A doctorate plus a law degree, and she didn't look older than twenty-six or seven.

John droned on listing Ben's credentials, including his degree in journalism from the University of Colorado at Boulder, his former job on the *Santa Fe Sun*, then his rise to fame in the past year as "Dear Ben."

La-di-da, Chapel thought. They made him sound like Wonder Boy. How tough was it to sit in front of a typewriter and produce that drivel?

"Dr. Barclay," John said.

"What?" she said crossly. "I mean, yes?"

"In your letter you stated that Ben Simmons is setting men and women back in their goal to be treated as equals. Would you care to elaborate?"

"Certainly," she said, sitting up straighter and tugging on her jacket lapels. "I believe neither men nor women wish to be viewed as sex objects. We are intelligent, independent human beings capable of activities outside of the bedroom." There was a smattering of applause from the audience, and Chapel smiled slightly. "Mr. Simmons," she continued, "insists on advising—"

"Call me Ben," he said.

"What?" She snapped her head around to look at him.

"Call me Ben, and I'll call you Chapel," he said,

flashing her a hundred-watt smile. "We're all friends here. You were saying, Chapel?"

No one should have a smile like that, she thought, tearing her gaze from Ben's face and redirecting her attention to John. No one!

"As I was saying," she said tightly, "Mr. Simmons's continual urging of men and women to use their bodies as a means of maintaining a relationship is degrading. Evenings centered on nothing more than seduction are not worthy of who all of us are today. Communication is the key; talking, sharing opinions, working out problems. Sex is not enough to cement the foundation between a man and woman."

"Sure can't hurt," Ben said, bringing a laugh from the audience. "Sorry," he added, as Chapel glared at him. "Didn't mean to interrupt. Go right ahead with your dissertation, counselor."

"A man," Chapel said, "should respect a woman for who she is, not the way she's built. Her accomplishments are far more important than her bra size!"

Ben laughed. He couldn't help himself. "Here we go. The brains-versus-breasts number."

"Mr. Simmons, *I* am speaking here," Chapel said. "Would you kindly wait your turn?"

"Of course, darlin'," he drawled. "I won't say another word."

"Ah-ha!" she cried, pointing her finger in the air. "There is a perfect example of what I'm referring to. What gives you the right to call me darlin' when you don't even know me? Have I called you honey or sweetie?"

"No, darn it," Ben said, snapping his fingers. "But a man can hope."

The audience roared with laughter, as Chapel pressed her lips together and gave Ben a murderous look.

Lighten up, Simmons, Ben told himself. Chapel darlin' was a breath away from tearing him limb from limb. Lord, she was something though. All fire and brimstone, cute as a button. Of course, *cute* was probably another word she'd do battle over. There was a lot of passion in that fragile little body, Ben mused. Angry passion at the moment, but what if it were channeled down the road of desire? She'd be dynamite!

"So," John was saying, "you feel, Dr. Barclay, that Mr. Simmons is leading men and women astray, undoing the progress that's been made in creating equality in society?"

"I certainly do," she said, nodding decisively.

"Thank you, Dr. Barclay. Mr. Simmons, your comment?"

"Chapel has unfortunately misinterpreted the purpose of my column. I am not advocating sex per se; I am reintroducing the element of romance. Candlelight dinners transmit the message that the other person is important, appreciated. We all need those kinds of strokes. Romance should always be present in a relationship, then everything else falls into its proper slot."

"You call wearing nothing but a red bow romantic?" Chapel asked, her voice rising.

"Oh, yes, ma'am," Ben said, grinning at her. "I most certainly do."

"It's demeaning," she said, folding her arms over her breasts.

"Out of context maybe it sounds a bit bizarre, but think about it a minute. It's the man's birthday. The woman could go spend a hundred dollars on him, but instead she gives him her most precious possession. Herself. She's saying that's how much she loves him. Yes, it's romantic, because there's nothing she can buy him that would be worth as much as herself, her love."

The audience went wild. They hooted and hollered, applauded exuberantly, and some even got to their feet to show their support of Ben's statement. Ben looked at Chapel steadily, waiting for the anger to show in the emerald depths of her eyes. But he saw something else, a flicker of an emotion he couldn't understand, nor put a name to. He frowned slightly as their gazes held, then Chapel turned away and stared down at her hands.

Damn him, she thought. He'd brainwashed the audience—the whole country, for that matter. He made the red bow caper sound like the dearest, sweetest, most romantic . . . Damn him! She might as well not bother to say another word. She'd lost the jury, she knew it, and was beaten. It had happened to her in the courtroom on occasion, and she recognized the signs. All she could do now was wait until this fiasco was over, then get out of there as quickly as possible.

The remainder of the show went as Chapel predicted. The questions from the audience and the home viewers who telephoned in were directed to Ben. They asked for advice regarding various troubled areas in their relationships, and his answers never strayed far from creating intimate settings, dressing provocatively, and luring the partner into a silken trap. The questions came from an almost even number of men and women.

"Mr. Simmons," John finally said, "suppose I asked you how to spice up my marriage? Do I, the man, greet my wife at the door wearing nothing but a red bow?"

The audience tittered, then grew silent to await Ben's answer. Chapel was on full alert.

"Absolutely," Ben said. "Red bow, or only a smile, it doesn't matter. The purpose is to bring romance back into your relationship, and we men have been remiss in that area. I have a tendency to give the initial, but only the initial, responsibility of romance to women because, let's face it, they're warm, caring, marvelous creatures who have a better understanding of sensitivity and tenderness. We men could, and should, take a lesson from them, then pick up the ball and do our share. Women are fantastic. I'd hate to go through life without them."

That did it, Chapel thought. Ben Simmons could run for president tomorrow and win! Oh, what a phony, cornball bunch of bull! Fancy words, to say that women were bubbleheads, who knew how to smoothe a man's furrowed brow before he took her to bed. What about her brain, her career, her accomplishments? Didn't anyone care?

In a rush of words John suddenly announced they were out of time, thanked Chapel and Ben for appearing on *Opposite Views*, and wished everyone a pleasant, prosperous, and ro-o-mantic day.

Chapel rolled her eyes to the heavens.

"Excellent," John said, beaming at Chapel and Ben.

"Slightly one-sided, wouldn't you say?" Chapel asked, getting to her feet.

"On the contrary," John said. "You made your points very well. That's what we present here, opposite views. Well, thanks again. Be sure and catch the show tomorrow, so you can see yourselves. Good-bye."

"Need a lift somewhere?" Ben asked Chapel as John walked away.

"No, thank you," she said, brushing past him.

"Hey, John was right. You did a good job, especially for your first time on television."

"Your approval just makes my day," she snapped, turning to face him.

"You really don't like me at all, do you?" he said, frowning. "Do you find romance that distasteful?"

"Romance? Mr. Simmons, you can use all your flowery words from here to Sunday to justify your preachings, but I still say you urge the use of a woman's body as a sex object to entice a man, and vice versa. No, I don't like you. Anyone with half a brain shouldn't like you. But you're taking care of that quite nicely. You're turning your readers' brains into shredded wheat topped with a big red bow. Just . . . take a hike!" She spun on her heel and marched away.

"Whew!" Ben said, a slow smile tugging onto his lips. "Yep, there's a helluva lot of passion in that nifty little body. A helluva lot!"

He walked back down the hall to the waiting room, where he shrugged into his overcoat and headed for the elevator. Outside the snow was falling even more heavily and was being whipped into swirling, stinging masses by a chill, biting wind. Ben glanced around for any sign of Chapel Barclay, but she was nowhere in sight.

"Ready to go, sir?" the driver of the limousine asked.

"What?" Ben said. "Oh, yeah, sure. Let's get out of this mess. Damn, it's cold."

Twenty minutes later Ben entered his hotel suite, shrugged out of his overcoat and jacket, then pulled his tie off and undid the two top buttons of his shirt. The flashing light on his telephone indicated he had a message, and he dialed the front desk. Minutes later Ben was speaking to his agent, Joe McBride, in New York.

"So? How'd it go?" Joe asked after they'd exchanged greetings.

"Okay," Ben said, stretching out on the bed. "The opposite view was a feminist lawyer who hates my guts."

"And the audience? How'd they swing?"

" 'Dear Ben' stole the show. The feminist didn't last five minutes."

"Good, good."

"I don't know, Joe. She really took it in the chops. She was trying to make a point, but no one even listened to her. What I picture as romance, she sees as sexual exploitation. It's valid reasoning on her part, but the audience didn't want any. I felt kind of sorry for her."

"Never waste sympathy on a nonfan. Hell, feminists

probably think Santa Claus is a chauvinist because his reindeer are all male."

"They are?"

"Yeah, I think so, but with names like that, who knows? Anyway, I'll catch the show tomorrow morning when it airs here. Have you decided yet if you want to come to New York for Christmas? I'm telling you, Ben, we'll do this town up royally."

"I don't know, Joe. I'm freezing my butt off here. My Santa Fe sunshine sounds very appealing."

"Yeah, but you said your folks are off on a cruise. Nobody should be alone on Christmas. Well, the offer stands. You've got two weeks to decide."

"I appreciate it. I'll let you know."

"Are you flying home today?"

"Yeah."

"If your weather looks like ours, you'd better call the airport first. Nothing is coming in or out of Kennedy. Well, I'll talk to you soon, Ben. Congrats on blitzing the libber. See ya."

"Okay, Joe. Bye." Ben slowly replaced the receiver. Blitzing? That had happened to him a hundred times when he'd been a quarterback on his college football team. Had he blitzed Chapel? Was it pain he had seen in her green eyes? She believed in something, and no one had listened to her. Yes, that could hurt. He'd blown holes in her theory by expressing his opinion, and he'd sincerely meant every word. Romance *was* important in a relationship, and he'd keep right on pushing for hot tubs and big red bows.

Why couldn't Chapel see the need for romance in this topsy-turvy world? he wondered, lacing his fingers under his head as he stared at the ceiling. Had she been burned in the past by a crummy lover? Or had she never loved at all? Had she been so busy getting her degrees that she hadn't had time to fit a man into her life? What, Ben asked himself, made Dr. Chapel Barclay tick?

Chapel. Pretty name, and a pretty woman. Loosen that hair, trade in the lawyer suit for something soft and feminine, and she'd be a knockout. Did that sound sexist? Well, hell, women looked him over too! They were just as guilty of judging a man by the way he looked and how he was built. It was how the game was played.

But he'd bet twenty bucks that Chapel didn't play the singles game. No, she wouldn't go in for sexually gratifying one-night stands. Not Chapel. She had class. She— Why was he thinking about that woman? For all he knew, she was married to a fat stockbroker, and they spent their time in bed discussing the state of the economy. No, she wasn't married. He'd put another twenty on it. Chapel in bed with a man? That was not a welcome image in his mind. Why not? What difference did it make to him whom she slept with? But imagine all that fiery anger turned into passion. Whoo-ee, that would be something!

"Enough!" Ben said, swinging his feet to the floor as a shaft of heat shot across the lower regions of his body. "Why am I thinking about Ms. Feminist, U.S.A.? I'll never see her again!"

Two

By the time Chapel entered her office building, she was exhausted. Driving from the television studio had been difficult in the blowing snow, and she had had to pull over to the curb several times to push the heavy snow off her windshield. She had refused the offer of the limousine provided for guests on *Opposite Views*, and after ten minutes of driving she'd regretted her decision.

Dr. Chapel Barclay was also furious!

As she replayed the television show in her mind her anger grew and was directed at one person. Ben Simmons. Cocky, arrogant, phony-as-a-three-dollar-bill Ben Simmons.

Chapel stepped into the elevator and shivered. The image of Ben danced before her eyes, and she frowned. There was nothing appealing about the man, she told herself. Nothing. His gorgeous eyes and hair, the wide set of his shoulders, that smile—oh, Lord, that smile that revealed teeth that were startlingly white against his handsome tanned face— were all trivial details, folderol. Ben Simmons was a sexist from the word go, and his attitudes and advice were enough to give her the screaming meemies! Big red bow, her big toe!

"Hello, hello," her secretary said, as Chapel entered her attractively furnished reception area.

"Coffee. Freezing," Chapel said, through chattering teeth.

"Oh, you poor dear. Go into your office. I'll bring it right in."

"Thank you, Beth."

Beth Kolb was a plump woman in her fifties with curly salt-and-pepper hair, a ready smile, and a quick mind that made her a top-notch secretary. When Chapel had opened her own office the previous year, Beth had applied for the job as secretary, stating she had had enough of the inner politics in the huge all-male law firm where she was working. The men, she declared, spent more time jockeying for position and preening their feathers than they did concentrating on their cases. Chapel had hired her on the spot.

In her office Chapel took off her coat and boots, then yanked her shoes out of the boots and dropped them on the floor. Sinking onto the soft leather sofa, she sighed, leaned her head back, and closed her eyes.

"Awful weather," Beth said, coming into the room. "Here, drink this while it's hot."

"Thank you," Chapel said, sitting up and accepting the mug of steaming coffee.

"So? How did it go?"

"Grim. Awful. Terrible. I despise that man! I detest that man! I can't stand that man!"

"It was love at first sight, huh?" Beth said, laughing merrily. "Is Ben Simmons really as good-looking in person as he is on magazine covers?"

"Disgustingly better."

"Really? He must be incredible."

"Oh, he's incredible, all right," Chapel said, scowling into her cup. "Incredibly sexist. Can you believe he justified the red-bow bit by saying it was romantic? That's the label he puts on all his sickening advice: romantic. He's smooth as glass, and the audience lapped it up like thirsty puppies. I didn't stand a chance. He even called me 'darlin' in this low, sexy voice. Darlin', for crying out loud!"

"Low, sexy voice? Matched up with those bedroom eyes? Oh, good heavens!"

"Puh-leeze, Beth," Chapel said, moaning. "Spare me. I don't wish to discuss Mr. Simmons any further. I just pray that anyone I know is busy working tomorrow morning when that show airs. I'm going to dismiss the whole thing from my mind and pretend it never happened."

"Okay . . . darlin'."

"Not funny! How long before my first appointment arrives?"

"There's no first appointment, or any others, for that matter. Everyone called and canceled because of this storm. The weather service is advising people to stay put. Schools are closing, and most businesses are sending employees home. I just caught the latest report on the radio. We're in for a beaut."

"I thought it was rather wild out there. Driving was next to impossible. I want you to go home, Beth."

"But I can get oodles of work done with no interruptions."

"No, you go on while the streets are still passable."

"What about you, Chapel?"

"Oh, I'm leaving, too, as soon as I gather some files to take with me. Believe me, I have no desire to spend the night here. Go! Don't try to come in tomorrow morning if it's this bad."

"Well, all right. Promise me you'll scurry out of here?"

"Yes, I'll scurry," Chapel said, smiling at her. "Bye."

"Good-bye. Hop into a warm bath the minute you get home to take off the chill."

"I will."

After Beth had left, Chapel walked to the window to stare out at the raging storm. It was almost frightening in its intensity, and she shivered as she wrapped her hands more tightly around her mug. She liked living in Detroit, with its changing seasons and varied activities, but on a day like today, she could easily daydream about sunny skies and warm temperatures, about places like Santa Fe.

"Santa Fe?" she said aloud. She'd never been there in her life. Why had she thought about a place— Ben Simmons! He was from Santa Fe. Why in heaven's name was she thinking of a city that was connected with 'Dear Ben'? Well, one thing was for sure. There were no planes leaving Detroit today. Ben darlin' was going to freeze his tush with the rest of them. She hoped his tan faded. Did westerners own winter boots and heavy coats? Oh, who cared if he froze to death? It would serve him right if he had to camp out on the floor of the airport. Surely he hadn't rented a car. He wouldn't know the first thing about driving in weather like this and— "Shut up, Chapel," she said. "You're mentally blithering. And you, Ben Simmons, get out of my head!"

With a snort of disgust Chapel reached for her briefcase and began to gather files she could study at home. Fifteen minutes later she flicked on the answering machine, pulled on her soggy coat and boots, and left the office.

By early afternoon Ben was pacing the floor of his sitting room. He'd eaten lunch in the hotel coffee shop, bought a newspaper and a paperback mystery, then returned to his room after being assured by the desk clerk that there was no problem with him keeping his reservation for longer than expected. He had read the newspaper, the book had not held his interest, there was nothing on television but gloomy weather reports, and Ben Simmons was going out of his mind!

Green eyes, cinnamon-colored hair, he thought, completing another circle of the room. Soft ivory skin, and such kissable lips. He kept seeing that flicker of pain in her pretty eyes too. It was his fault. No, it wasn't! The audience could have swung the other way just as easily, totally supporting Chapel's viewpoint. He had no control over the public, or their opinions. Chapel had gone on that show by choice, and should have been prepared to take her lumps. That was, after all, equal rights.

Why was she haunting him like this? It was the weather. He was cooped up like a caged animal. No, it was the woman. He might as well admit it and quit playing mind games. So now what? How was he going to rid himself of this nagging guilt about what had happened to Chapel on that show?

"Call her," he suggested aloud. Oh, really? And say what? "Hi, Chapel. How's show biz?" Dumb. Well, he'd wing it. He'd say hello, test out her mood, and take it from there. If she was still mad as hell, he'd dust her off. But what if she sounded sad, sort of defeated . . . beaten . . . blitzed?

"Hell," he said, reaching for the telephone book. "She's driving me nuts!"

Not good, Ben thought a few minutes later as he hung up the phone. He'd gotten a recorded message when he'd called Chapel's office. Some grandmotherly-sounding woman had said to leave a message at the beep, which he hadn't done. Had Chapel left work because of the weather, or was she that upset after the show? Had to be the weather, because the grandmother was gone too. Right? Right. Unless . . . Granny had to take a totally distraught Chapel home!

"Oh, good Lord!" Ben said, getting to his feet. No, he told himself, Chapel was tough. She was a liberated woman, a successful attorney, a . . . fragile, beautiful woman, who had gotten in over her head today because of him. He just needed to know she was okay!

He found a listing for C. Barclay in the white pages, and after hesitating a moment dialed the number shown. When no ringing started on the other end of the line, he dialed again. Still no ring. He then asked the operator to put him through, and was told that the number was temporarily out of order, probably due to the blizzard.

"Wonderful," he muttered, drumming his fingers on the nightstand. "Just wonderful."

With his jaw clenched tightly, he scribbled Chapel's address on a piece of paper, grabbed his topcoat, and strode from the room.

Chapel sank up to her chin in a lilac-scented bubblebath and sighed with pleasure. Oh, the warm water was heavenly, she thought. As much as she would have preferred to come straight home, she knew the empty state of her kitchen cupboards and had stopped at the grocery store. Half of Detroit, it seemed, had decided to stock their pantries in case they became housebound, and the lines at the checkout had been long. Three hours after leaving the office, she had at last entered her apartment, put the groceries away, and headed for a hot tub.

"Oh, no!" she said, as a knock sounded at her apartment door. "Not now!" Darn it, she fumed. She pulled the plug and stepped out of the tub onto a fluffy bathmat. She could no more ignore a knock at the door than she could a ringing telephone.

After drying quickly, she pulled on a rose-colored

satin robe and tugged the sash around her waist. She had swept her hair up onto the top of her head and secured it with a few randomly placed pins. Some tendrils had pulled loose, and she brushed at them irritably as she walked into the living room.

"I'm coming!" she called as another solid thud reverberated against her door. "Have a little patience!"

She flung the door open, then just stood there, staring at the tall figure before her. The Abominable Snowman had arrived at her apartment! It was enormous! It was covered in snow and ice, including its face, was shaking from head to foot, and it was growling!

"Aaak!" Chapel screamed, her hands flying to her cheeks.

"Errr!" the monster said, slowly lifting a snow covered arm.

"Aaak!"

"Ch . . . ap . . . el," the thing rumbled.

"Good grief! It knows my name!" she yelled. "Go away! Go away!"

"B . . . B . . . Ben!"

"Ben?" she whispered. "Dear Ben? Ben Simmons? You're Ben Simmons?"

"Errr," it said, nodding slightly.

A door farther down the hall popped open, and a woman stuck her head out.

"What's all the racket?" she yelled. "I'm trying to watch my soaps. Go play Frosty the Snowman somewhere else!"

"Ben," Chapel said, grabbing his arm, "come in here quick, before she calls the police or something."

"Fro . . . zen," he said. He moved forward with jerky steps, reminding Chapel of a robot.

"Ben, why are you frozen?" she asked, closing the door after they were inside. "And why are you here? What do you want?"

"Oh my God, I'm dying!" Ben said. "P-pull my coat off, will you?"

"Oh, yes, of course," she said, working the heavy, sodden material down Ben's back and arms.

A burgundy-colored sweater came into view, then jeans that fit snugly over narrow hips and tight buttocks. Chapel swallowed heavily, then, staggering slightly under the weight of the coat, marched into the bathroom and heaved it over the shower rod. When she returned to the living room, Ben Simmons was sitting on her sofa, taking off his shoes and socks.

"What are you doing?" she asked, her eyes widening.

"Blocks of ice. My feet are lousy blocks of ice! Ow! They hurt, like pins sticking in them. Is that a sign of frostbite? I swear, this city is a death trap! I could have frozen stiff out there in an upright position, and someone probably would have hung a Christmas tree ornament on me. Do you have any whiskey? Brandy? I'll settle for cheap rum, anything to thaw out my insides. I have never in my life been so cold!"

"I . . . yes, okay," Chapel said. She hurried into the kitchen and returned with a snifter of brandy. "There," she said. "Why are you here?"

"Oh, that feels good going down," Ben said, after taking a deep swallow of the liquor. "I may live. But then again, I may not. May my death be on your conscience, Chapel Barclay. This is all your fault!"

"Mine?" she planted her hands on her hips. "Did I invite you here? No. Do I know what I've done to deserve the dubious honor of your presence? No. Did I ask you to turn yourself into a six-foot Popsicle? No, I did not! Go home, Ben Simmons!"

"Can't. Planes aren't flying." He drained his glass. "Ah-h-h, that hit the spot. Do you know that the cab driver pulled over to the curb three blocks from here and walked away? Can you believe that? He said he wasn't driving another foot in this garbage. There I was, left alone to hoof it. I guess you can lay some of the guilt for my death on the cab driver if you want to. You have to accept your share though. My toes hurt. Is that normal?"

"I—"

"Oh, Chapel," he said, his voice suddenly husky, "my brain just defrosted. You look sensational in that robe, and I really like your hair. You are a beautiful, beautiful woman, Chapel Barclay."

Chapel's heart did a strange little tap dance, and she became acutely aware that she was naked beneath her robe. Ben's yummy dark eyes seemed to be seeing right through the material and warming her flesh beneath. His gaze drifted over her, then up to lock onto her eyes, pinning her in place.

She was beautiful? she asked herself silently. She was? Oh, she was not! she thought, snapping herself back to reality. That was flash and dash Ben Simmons talking. "Dear Ben," of big red bow fame. Why was he sitting in her apartment in his bare feet?

"Why are you here?" she asked. "And this time I'd like a nice precise answer."

"I was worried about you," he said, smiling at her as he spread his arms out across the top of the sofa. "Don't you want to sit down?"

"No! Worried? About me? Why?"

"I don't know, Chapel," he said, frowning slightly. "I just couldn't get that TV show off my mind. You got a bum rap, and I wanted to make sure you were all right. Being blitzed is no picnic."

"Blitzed? That means drunk."

"Not always. Anyway, I'm sorry about how things went. I tried to reach you at your office, but your grandmother was on the answering machine, so I came here. Your phone is out of order, by the way."

She shook her head, then squinted at Ben. "I'm not positive that I understood a word of that," she said. "My grandmother? I don't have a grandmother. You turned yourself into a human icicle because of what happened on *Opposite Views*?"

"Yep," he said, looking rather pleased with himself. "I took on the ravages of the storm and lived to tell about it . . . I think. If certain parts of my anatomy no longer function, I'm going to sue the city of Detroit. I've heard of cold showers, but this is ridiculous!"

It was too much. It really was. The whole thing was just so absurd that Chapel burst into laughter. She sank onto a chair, gasping for breath, looked at Ben, then fell apart again.

"What the hell is so funny?" he finally asked crossly.

She took a deep breath, cleared her throat, and plastered a semiserious expression on her face.

"Sorry," she said. "It's just rather cuckoo, if you think about it. Why would anyone in their right mind freeze their . . . person for someone who despises them?"

"Do you, Chapel?" he asked, his voice seeming to drop an octave. "Do you despise me?"

Like black velvet, she thought. His voice was as soft and rich as black velvet—stroking, caressing, her. "I—" she began, a slight tremor in her own voice, "I don't know you personally, Ben. It's your column, the things you say, the advice you give. It's against every principle I base my life on."

"You're that much opposed to romance? Why?"

"Romance? Do you honestly believe that?"

"Yes, I do. Chapel, I inherited that advice column and had no intention of continuing with it. Then I really started reading the mail, hearing the loneliness, the frustration, and the unhappiness those people were pouring out on paper. They were so desperate, they were willing to ask for help from a stranger. I've tried my damnedest to give them what they want, need: Love. What's wrong with recapturing that glorious feeling when love first hits you? Just because two people have been together for a while doesn't mean the excitement should be over."

"So the woman meets the man at the door decked out in a red bow?"

"Satin robes are nice too," he said, flashing her a dazzling smile.

"Men and women have more to offer than just their bodies, Ben Simmons," she said, her voice rising.

"Hell, I know that!"

"Do you? I wonder. Which would you prefer to do? Go to bed with me or sit here and talk?"

"That is the dumbest question I've heard in my entire life. Let's go in the bedroom."

"Ah-ha! I rest my case."

"Hey, I'm a normal, healthy, red-blooded male. I am sitting close to a very beautiful woman, who is wearing only a clinging satin robe that hides little. What do you think I am? A candidate for sainthood? Hell, yes, I'd like to make love to you, but that doesn't make me a sex maniac. And for your information, I'd enjoy talking to you, too, getting to know who you are, what makes you tick. There are many forms of communication, Chapel. Sex is one. It's a very important element in a relationship, but talking, laughing, crying with someone are just as important."

Chapel opened her mouth, shook her head, then closed her mouth. "I think," she finally said, "I'll have to digest your dissertation. I . . . um, believe I'll get dressed."

"Why? Because I said how you look in that robe? Whom are you afraid of? Me? Or you?"

"Knock it off," she said, getting to her feet.

"I can't figure out where you're coming from," he said, raking a hand through his thick hair. "What have you got against romance? Against men? Against me? If you were unattractive I could see it as a subconscious rationale, because you'd be protecting yourself from rejection. Hell, Chapel, you're a beautiful, very desirable woman. So okay, you're a superbrain, but does that mean you have to deny your own sexuality, your femininity? It just doesn't make sense!"

"Deny my— You have no idea what you're talking about! You don't even know me!"

"I know you're the woman who wants my column banned because I advocate romance, making love, the whole nine yards. That tells me a helluva lot about you. What turns you on? An in-depth discussion about the stock market?"

"Aaah!" she screamed. Ben jerked in surprise. "You're despicable. Get out of my house! Now! This minute!"

"It's cold outside!"

"Tough tootsies, buster. I want you to haul it out of here!"

"No!"

"I'll call the police!"

"Your phone isn't working, if you recall. I nearly died coming over here out of genuine concern for your emotional well-being, Chapel Barclay. I'll be damned if I'm going back out in that death trap. Nope. I'm staying. That's it."

"You certainly are not!"

"Go put some clothes on before I ravish your body," he said, glaring at her.

"Ravish my body?" A bubble of laughter escaped from her lips. "I thought only pirates did that. Is that before or after you jump my bones?"

Ben shook his head and laughed softly. "You are something, Chapel. You're screaming like a banshee one minute, then you fill the room with your sunshiny laughter the next. You're hard to keep track of."

"Then don't try!" she snapped, heading for the bedroom. "I'm getting dressed, due to the fact that I'm freezing."

Ben cringed as the bedroom door slammed with a reverberating thud.

Whew! he thought. Chapel was in a real snit again. All that heavenly passion being used up in anger. Well, he *had* gotten a bit mouthy, telling her she was denying her femininity. That had not been the swiftest move of his life. Now she was mad as hell. But then he remembered her laughter. It had come out of the blue, and her face had lit up. Her green eyes had sparkled like emeralds. A very complex woman was Dr. Chapel Barclay. She really didn't see the difference between romance and sexual exploitation. Hadn't she ever been courted, made to feel like the most special woman on earth? No, probably not. She'd examine every move a guy made for any hint of overt sexist activities. Liberation was fine, but Chapel was overdoing it!

Chapel was carrying on a nonstop muttered conversation with herself regarding the less than flattering attributes of Mr. Ben Simmons. As she reached in her drawer for clean underwear, she glimpsed her reflection in the full-length mirror, and turned for a better view.

Was she a beautiful, desirable woman? Average, maybe, but definitely not beautiful. Oh, forget it. Ben Simmons had his smooth delivery down to an art. He worked a little verbal seduction on his prey before getting to the nitty-gritty. Lord, the man had a lot of nerve. The very idea of saying she denied her own sexuality! She certainly did not! Just because she wasn't into bed-hopping didn't mean she didn't like being a woman. An independent, intelligent, liberated woman. If a man wasn't interested in her brains along with her . . . other assets, he could just forget it! So there!

"So there?" she asked herself. "How mature. What's next? I stamp my foot and stick out my tongue?" Enough of that, she thought, pulling on her jeans. She'd better direct her attention to the problem at hand. Ben Simmons was still in her living room in his bare feet, and apparently had no intention of leaving! Just how long did he think he was going to stay? A hour? Two? Four? The whole night? Oh, ha! She had news for Mr. Simmons. Snow or no snow, he was going to shuffle off to Buffalo right now!

Chapel finished dressing in a bulky knit green sweater, then pushed her feet into gigantic fuzzy purple slippers. She pulled the pins from her hair and brushed it free, allowing the auburn tresses to tumble past her shoulders in gentle waves.

"Definitely average," she said, wrinkling her nose at her reflection in the mirror. "Oh, well, that's how it goes. Okay, Ben darlin', gear up! You are tooling off to Tulsa!"

Ben caught a glimpse of something zooming past as Chapel left her bedroom and disappeared into the kitchen.

"Good-bye, Ben," she called. "Drop by again in ten or twenty years."

Purple feet? Ben wondered, getting up from the sofa. Great big purple feet? No, he must have imagined it.

"You're supposed to be gone," Chapel said crossly when he appeared in the kitchen doorway.

"They *are* purple!" he said, his gaze riveted on her slippers.

"What? Oh, yes. They're very cozy. Good-bye."

Ben chuckled, folded his arms across his chest, and leaned against the doorjamb. The light was beginning to dawn. Chapel Barclay had absolutely no idea how appealing and attractive she was! Right now, in her tight jeans and a sweater that matched her eyes, with that silky cascade of hair she was fantastic. Hell, she even looked good with giant economy-size purple feet!

"Ben," Chapel said. "Benjamin. Is your name Benjamin?"

"Yep. Benjamin William Simmons. Classy, huh?"

"Outstanding. Look, I've had a very trying day. I'd appreciate it if you'd kindly leave so I can relax and rejuvenate myself."

"Rejuvenate yourself?" he said, grinning at her. "How does one go about doing that? That sounds a little kinky, Chapel."

"I don't give a tinker's damn what it sounds like, Ben-ja-min! Get out of my house!" Damn the man! And damn that bone-melting smile!

"Chapel, be reasonable. Even the cab drivers are abandoning ship. Nothing is moving in this town, and I can't possibly get back to my hotel. Hey, do you know some guy in this building who would let me crash on his sofa tonight?"

"No."

"Oh, that's a shame," he said, an expression of pure innocence on his face. "Well, the only liberated, humanitarian thing for you to do is let me stay here.

Do not forget, counselor, I came through rain, sleet, and gloom of night to check up on your mental cool."

"It was snow you came through," she said, frowning at him. "Snow, which may have stopped and be totally melted by now."

"Good point. Let us venture to yon window and peer forth."

"The window in my bedroom looks out over the street," she said. "I'll go look."

Ben watched as Chapel left the kitchen, then looked around the small room. The main color was yellow, and everything was immaculately clean, with nothing out of place. He wandered back into the living room and his gaze traveled over the furnishings. Done in earth tones of brown, orange, and yellow, the room was homey and comfortable, but something was missing. There was, he realized, no personal touches, no knickknacks, pictures in frames, no favorite magazines on the coffee table. It was as though no one had yet moved in to add the special touches that would make the room hers alone.

"Ben!" Chapel called from the bedroom. "Come in here a minute."

"Best offer I've had all day," he said under his breath.

Chapel was standing at the windows, her arms wrapped tightly around herself. Ben came up behind her, resisting the urge to pull her back against him and mold her soft body to his. He settled for inhaling her fresh, feminine aroma.

"Ben, look," she said, her voice hushed. "You can't see farther than a few inches. The snow is beating against the window and it's like everything has disappeared. The city, the people . . . I've never seen anything quite like this before. It's like a sci-fi movie where we've been lifted away, deposited someplace else, and we don't even know it."

"You sound a little frightened," he said, tentatively lifting his hands and placing them on her shoulders.

"It's . . . eerie."

"You could be right, you know. We're the only two people left, just you and me." He slowly turned her to face him. "Would that be so terrible, Chapel?"

"Ben . . ."

"Don't be afraid of me," he said, cradling her face in his hands. "I won't hurt you. I would never do anything to hurt you."

"You're going to kiss me, aren't you?" she asked, hearing the breathlessness in her own voice.

"Yes, I am," he said, his thumbs trailing lazy circles over her pale cheeks.

"Why would you want to kiss someone who doesn't even like you?"

"Chapel?"

"Yes?"

"You talk too much," he said, and lowered his mouth to hers.

He brushed his lips over hers lightly, fleetingly, then in the next instant gathered her close to his chest as the kiss intensified. Of their own volition, it seemed, Chapel's hands wrapped around his neck, and she parted her lips to his insistent tongue.

A wonderous trembling began deep within Chapel and traveled throughout her. Ben's hands roamed over her back, and their heat seeped through her sweater and made her skin tingle. She leaned against him, savoring the strength, the feel of his powerful body. Her breasts grew taut, aching, as desire shot through her. And the kiss went on and on.

Ben lifted his head to draw a raspy breath, then took possession of her lips again, drinking in the sweetness of her mouth. Her full breasts were crushed against his chest, and the sweet, natural scent of her body was intoxicating, drugging his senses. His hands slid to her buttocks, and he pulled her up to him, fitting her hips to his, his arousal hard against her. He groaned deep in his throat as her tongue met his, and a tremor of desire swept through him.

"Chapel," he murmured, trailing kisses down the slender column of her neck. "Oh, Chapel, I knew you'd feel like this in my arms. You're so beautiful, darlin'."

Darlin'? she thought, stiffening in his arms as she snapped out of her hazy state. Darlin'!

Uh-oh, Ben thought, drawing a steadying breath. He'd blown it. *Darlin'* was not Chapel's all-time favorite word.

"Chapel, I—"

"Get your big paws off me, Ben Simmons!" she said, wiggling out of his arms and praying her voice was steady. "I am not, nor will I ever be, your darlin'! You're despicable!"

"Ah, hell. Again?" he asked, raking his hand through his hair.

"Still! You never stopped being despicable!"

He grinned. "I took time off to kiss you."

"Oh, no, you don't! Don't smile that sexy smile at me, you . . . you . . ."

"You think I have a sexy smile? I'll be damned." He reached for her again.

"Get out of my bedroom!"

"You invited me in here!"

"I'm *uninviting* you. Go!"

"Chapel, don't you think you're overreacting a bit to a simple little word?"

"*Darlin'* is not just a word. It's an attitude, a demeaning, degrading attitude. It's like *honey, baby, sweet cakes.*"

He burst into laughter. "Sweet cakes?"

"Definitely despicable," she said, and flounced out of the room, her purple slippers slapping against the carpet.

"Sweet cakes?" Ben repeated, still grinning. "Lord!"

He started after her, then stopped to survey the bedroom. Again there were no personal momentos, no frivolous figurines, nothing whimsical or fun. Shaking his head, he walked slowly from the room, a frown replacing his smile.

Three

It was not difficult for Ben to locate Chapel. The racket she was making in the kitchen was deafening.

"I'd hate to live next door to you," Ben said, strolling in and leaning against the counter. "Why are you killing those pots and pans? By the way, how do you want to divide up the chores?"

"Chores? What chores?" she asked, a pan in one hand, the lid in the other.

"Dinner. I'm a man of the eighties, Dr. Barclay. I have no qualms about doing my share in the kitchen. Since this is your home, I'll let you divvy things up. What are we having?"

"This isn't happening to me," Chapel said to the

pan. "It's all a nightmare, the alarm will go off, I'll wake up. There isn't a barefoot chauvinist standing in my kitchen demanding to know what's for dinner."

"I didn't demand! I simply asked a perfectly reasonable question, and I volunteered my services. In the kitchen. Helping with dinner. Don't hit me with that pan! I bruise very easily."

Chapel smacked the pan and lid onto the counter with a reverberating clang, then crossed her arms over her breasts.

"I would appreciate it, Mr. Simmons," she said in a low voice, "if you would please leave me alone for a minute so I can calmly, coolly, and rationally gather my data pertaining to this ludicrous situation and determine the appropriate course of action."

"Well—"

"Go into the living room!" she yelled.

"All right!" he said, making a hasty exit.

"That's better," she said, then sank into a chair at the table. What in heaven's name was she going to do? She couldn't throw Ben out. He'd freeze to death! There was no way possible he could get back to his hotel in that weather. No doubt people all over Detroit were putting folks up for the night because they couldn't make it home. But they didn't have barefoot Ben Simmons! When he had kissed her she had melted, just fallen apart. Never in her entire life had she responded to a man's kiss the way she had to Ben's.

"Crazy," she muttered. "I don't even like him!" But, oh, when he held her and kissed her, strange and wonderous things had happened. Desire like none before had swirled within her, making her feel alive, so very aware of her own femininity. Why? Why Ben? His attitudes were everything she despised in a man. Dear Ben was a menace to society! He was also dangerous as hell to be alone with in her apartment!

Now, hold it! she told herself sternly. This was dumb. She wasn't some naive, awed groupie of Ben Simmons's! She was a mature, intelligent woman who controlled her own destiny. So what if she had fallen prey to one of Ben's mind-boggling, toe-curling kisses? It didn't mean a thing. He'd caught her off-guard, but she was wise to him now and it wouldn't happen again. She could handle this. She'd be a Good Samaritan, give him refuge from the storm, then send him packing. No problem.

With a decisive nod Chapel got to her feet and marched into the living room as fast as her furry purple feet allowed her to.

"Mr. Simmons," she said, in a no-nonsense voice.

"Yes?" he said, smiling at her engagingly.

"I have decided that due to the inclement weather, I have little choice but to allow you to remain here until morning. However! Do make note that my offer includes food and the use of my sofa. That's it! There will be no hanky-panky!"

"Hanky-panky? I swear, counselor, you certainly do have a way with words."

"Are you listening to me?" she asked, planting her hands on her hips.

"I understand perfectly," he said, suppressing a smile. "I do! Really! I'll be the original Boy Scout. I can't begin to tell you how grateful I am. It's enough to bring tears to my eyes when I realize I won't be forced to crawl through the snow, feeling the strength ebb from my body, seeing my life flash before my eyes as I slowly lose conscious—"

"Put a cork in it," she said, spinning around and going back into the kitchen. "You can set the table."

"Yes, ma'am," he said, following close behind. "Whatever you say, ma'am. I aim to please."

Chapel's snort of disgust made Ben chuckle. Chapel Barclay was something, he thought as he carefully set the table. That kiss they had shared had been unbelievable! She was a passionate woman. She was complicated, too, like an intricate puzzle that was difficult to figure out. She presented herself as the epitome of the modern, career-oriented woman, in charge of her own life, needing no man to complete her world. She was a crusader for equal rights, a feminist from the word go. But beneath that veneer was another Chapel Barclay, a contradiction in goofy purple slippers. A woman whose eyes reflected hurt and vulnerability. A Chapel Barclay who had evoked desire within him of an indescribable intensity. When he had taken her into his arms, he had not wanted to let her go!

Ben finished setting the table, then turned around. He collided with two fuzzy purple feet that caught him square in the stomach.

"Oomph!" he said. "What in the . . . ?"

Chapel was kneeling on the counter peering into the cupboard. Ben reached up, placed his large hands around her waist, and set her back on her feet on the floor.

"Hey," she said. "I was looking for something up there!"

"Tell me what it is, and I'll get it down for you."

"I am perfectly capable of retrieving my belongings from my own cupboards, Mr. Simmons."

"I don't doubt that for a minute, Dr. Barclay. However, those purple feet of yours are lethal weapons, and I did inform you that I bruise easily. A man has the right to protect himself."

"Oh, for Pete's sake, all right," she said, frowning. "It's a clear bowl with scalloped edges. I'm going to make a tossed salad."

"Madam," Ben said, then sniffed indignantly. "I am perfectly capable of making a salad. Do you think that because I'm a man, I can only do the manual labor, like setting the table? Really, Chapel, I'm surprised at you."

"So make the salad! I don't care!"

"Great," he said, rubbing his hands together. "Where's the junk I get to chop up?"

"Good grief." She opened the refrigerator and pulled out an assortment of vegetables. "There," she said, plunking them on the counter. "Have a wonderful time. I'll— What did you do to the napkins?"

"Like that? A fold here, a tuck there, and, ta-da, a flower. My mom showed me how to do that when I was a kid laid up with the measles. I can make outstanding things out of paper napkins. I do a giraffe that you wouldn't believe. Having a man put a flower by your plate doesn't offend you, does it? Heaven knows, I wouldn't want to do that."

"No. No, of course, not," she said, picking up the napkin. "It's very pretty. I think I'll leave these like they are, and set out two more."

"Whatever," he said, concentrating on slicing a tomato as a smile tugged onto his lips.

A short time later they sat down to a meal of steak, salad, and hot rolls.

"Looks fantastic," Ben said. "*Is* fantastic," he added a moment later after taking a bite of steak. "You're a good cook."

"You did your share. The salad is delicious. I see you made flowers out of the radishes too."

"Yep. I'm really into flowers. So tell me: What do you do for fun?"

"Fun?"

"Yeah, you know, the weekend comes, it's time to kick back and enjoy. Fun. I assume you date."

"Yes, I do. I see a variety of men. We go to concerts, lectures, the theater."

"Mmm."

"What does 'mmm' mean?"

"Oh, nothing. You don't go to the Lions' football games?"

"And watch grown men beating each other up like little boys on the playground? No, thank you."

"Mmm."

"Darn it, Ben, quit making that noise! If you have something to say, say it."

"Well, I was just thinking that you have all the seasons here, unlike Santa Fe. Haven't you ever had a date in winter to build a snowman? Gone tromping through the leaves in autumn? Had a guy take you through the park in the spring to see the new flowers? Then in summer—"

"No," she interrupted quietly. "I've never done those things with anyone."

"Why not?" he asked, reaching across the table and covering her hand with his.

"The men I know wouldn't dream of . . . That is, they . . . They're other attorneys who—"

"Who only see you for your brains and take you on outings befitting your intellectual level. That's very chauvinistic of them, Chapel," Ben said, stroking her hand with his thumb.

"What? Why?" she asked. How could a man with bare feet have such a warm hand? she wondered wildly, as he stroked her hand with his thumb. She could feel the heat traveling up her arm, across her breasts, and— Heavens! Well, she was going to take her hand back! In a minute. "Answer the question."

"You strongly advocate the theory that men should view a woman for her brains, not just her breasts. Well, a guy who zeroes in on the brains and ignores the . . . other assets of a woman doesn't see her as a total entity either, and is also guilty of being narrow-minded. Get it?"

"That's ridiculous."

"It is not! Why does it have to be a trade-off? Why can't you enjoy your femininity to the hilt and be respected for your smarts as well?"

"It doesn't work that way," she said, finally pulling her hand from beneath his. "A woman can't dress like a femme fatale and still be treated as an equal in a male-oriented society."

"Then you're hanging out with the wrong males. I saw you in your lawyer clothes during the TV show. Now here you are in your purple feet and jeans with your hair hanging free. Does that change you into a dumb-dumb? Hell, no! It gives you more depth. I'm getting a glimpse of the complete Chapel Barclay and, believe me, I like what I see."

Chapel's heart did a strange hop, skip, and jump, then settled into a seminormal cadence. Ben was looking at her steadily, and there was no mockery, no amusement, in his dark eyes. Instead, she saw warmth and tenderness. She sifted his words through her mind, then shook her head slowly, tearing her gaze from his.

"Your theory just doesn't work," she said. "To be treated as an equal, I must dress as a counterpart to my male colleagues."

"Mmm," Ben said, spearing a radish with his fork.

Chapel glared at him.

They ate in silence, each lost in his own thoughts, then Ben got up and poured coffee for both of them.

"Delicious meal," he said. "Thank you."

"You're welcome, but you did do your share."

"It was your food though. I owe you a dinner. Oh, and after tomorrow morning I'll owe you a breakfast. If I can't leave then, I'll owe you—"

"Snow melts," she said, frowning at him. "And we have plows. Marvelous inventions. Detroit will be perking right along by daybreak."

Ben chuckled. "Trying to get rid of me, are you?"

"Yes! I mean no! Well, let's face it, having a perfect stranger spend the night is not my usual mode of conduct."

"I hate to break this to you," he said, grinning at her, "but I'm not perfect. Even my mother figured that out when I was two or three minutes old. Close, you understand, but not quite perfect."

"Forget I mentioned it," she said, bursting into laughter. "Your ego is incredible."

"I love it when you laugh," he said. "That is a pretty, pretty sound."

Their eyes met, and Chapel felt a tingling sensation feather up her spine. Her gaze skittered to Ben's lips, then back to his eyes. Those lips, she thought dreamily. Oh, yes, she remembered those lips. They were so soft, so sensuous; they had stirred something deep within her when they'd covered hers. The kiss she had shared with Ben had been like none before. And right now he was doing nothing more than looking at her, yet she felt as though she were drowning in the depths of those compelling dark eyes. Every inch of Ben Simmons shouted his vibrant charisma, virility. He was definitely, *definitely*, dangerous!

"Have you ever been in love?" she asked suddenly, breaking the eerie spell that had fallen. What? her mind asked. Where had that come from?

"Huh?" Ben said, shaking his head slightly. What had happened? he wondered. Chapel had gazed at him with those green eyes of hers, and he'd lost track of time, been unable to move. An hour could have passed, and he'd never have known it. What was it about her?

"In love," she repeated. "You write a column, often centering on advice to the lovelorn. Do you consider yourself an expert on the subject of love?"

"Hardly. But I was in love once. It was great, a nice place to be."

"What happened?"

"Nothing earth-shattering. We were in college, then graduated. She got a job offer as a translator and went to Italy. We spent a fortune on long-distance calls for several months, then tapered off, and eventually stopped. She married an Italian. I get a Christmas card from her every year. She's got four kids and she's happy. I like her a lot, and respect her. The whole episode taught me a great deal about myself, and I'm grateful to her for that. I think love is marvelous."

"But you haven't been in love since?"

"Nope. It just hasn't happened, but I'm hoping I'll get another shot at it. What about you? Have you been in love?"

"I don't think so."

"You don't know?"

"I was so young when I knew Clifford; just barely twenty. You see, I was always a loner because I never fit in. I was a freshman in college when I was fifteen. Clifford was older, a professor I met in my senior year. I think he was fascinated by me, and I was so hungry for attention. No, it wasn't love. I'm not bitter, just wiser. He was a very nice man, but I had no concept of what love was."

"Why not? Didn't your parents have a good marriage?"

"They were divorced when I was four. I never saw my father again. My mother was ahead of her time. She was liberated before it was fashionable. She's a very talented photographer. At the moment she's on a safari in Africa. She raised me to rely on my brains and to look out for myself. She always said that if I needed help to do something, then don't do it. 'Stand on your own two feet,' was the key phrase."

"Whew," Ben said, shaking his head. "That's cold. I don't mean to say anything derogatory about your mother, but that philosophy stinks! Everybody needs someone at various points in their life. There was this woman who worked at the paper with me in Santa Fe, who was my best friend. Austin and I saw each other through the good times and bad, until she got married and moved to Paris. She and I were there for each other, no questions asked. Still are, really."

"You're very fortunate," Chapel said quietly. "I've never had a best friend."

"Then you definitely haven't been in love."

"What do you mean?"

"Friendship is very important between lovers. Contrary to what you think I say in my column, I don't believe for one minute that sex is the focal point in a relationship. Oh, it's important, but if that's all there is, you don't have a helluva lot going for you. You have to toss in laughing and crying, sharing. I sure wish I had been in love when my cat died."

"What?"

"I had this great cat named Magnum P.I.G. He ate all the time. Anyway, I got him from a litter that Austin's cat, George, had. I swear, my Piggy was the smartest cat in Santa Fe. He got hit by a car, though, and was killed. I was a wreck. I even called Austin in Paris to tell her. She felt awful about it, but it wasn't the same as having someone I could be with, someone who would cry with me because they loved me that much. Damn, I sure did like that cat."

Ben frowned and stared at a spot on the wall above Chapel's head. She looked at him intently, studying the rather wistful expression on his face.

What a complicated man, she thought. She had never met anyone like him before. He was so big and strong, yet had no qualms about revealing his need for a special someone to share his life. He'd wanted to be held and comforted when his cat died? Was that weird? No, it was . . . dear, sweet. And lovers were also friends? Really?

"Do you play gin rummy?" he asked suddenly.

"What? Oh, no, I don't."

"Darn."

"Well, time to clean up," she said, getting to her feet. "I have some files to study."

"You work in the evenings?"

"Usually. I'll rinse the dishes, you load them into the dishwasher."

"Okay. Will it disturb your concentration if I watch TV?"

"I don't think so."

"We'll check it out. It's really a shame that you don't play gin rummy. It's a great game."

"I have a child-custody case coming up in court that I have to prepare for. The poor woman is falling apart because her ex-husband is trying to obtain custody of their five-year-old son."

"And?"

"And I'm going to win. That man doesn't want the boy. He's just angry, trying to hurt the woman any way he can because she divorced him."

"How do you know that?"

"I talked to him. It came through loud and clear. In addition, he didn't show up half the time for his visitation rights. His son is not high on his list of priorities."

"And *your* father, Chapel?" Ben asked quietly. "Why didn't he come to see you when you were growing up?"

She shrugged and started rinsing the dishes. "My mother said he remarried and had a large family. I guess he didn't feel the need to see me. The only memory I have of him is sitting on his lap when he read me a story. I don't know why I remember that, but I do."

"Did your mother read you stories after he left?"

"No. Well, I learned to read very early so there wasn't any need."

"Ahh, yes, the do-it-yourself number," Ben said as he finished filling the dishwasher. "Is your mother going to be back in time for Christmas?"

"Heavens no. She'll be gone for months. Whom do you spend Christmas with?"

"My parents. They went on a cruise this year though. I was really tickled for them. They've waited a long time for this. I assured them that Santa Claus would find me even if they were away."

"You probably really said that," Chapel said, smiling at him.

"I did!"

"Figures. One clean kitchen. Aren't your feet cold?"

"Are you offering to lend me your purple slippers?"

"Never. These are my pride and joy. I adore these slippers," she said, walking into the living room.

"Lucky slippers," he said under his breath, following her out of the kitchen.

In the living room Ben turned on the television with the volume low, then sat on the sofa at the opposite end from Chapel. She had retrieved several files from her briefcase, along with a legal-size pad, and was deeply engrossed in the material. Ben's gaze swept over her, her delicate features, her breasts pushing against the green sweater, the enticing curves of her hips. He recalled again the way her body had molded to his when he'd kissed her, and the sweet, sweet taste of her lips on his. As a coil of heat shot through him, he shifted slightly and cleared his throat.

Well, now, he thought, wasn't this cozy? A quiet evening at home with the little woman. Actually it was nice to relax for a change, and very nice not to be alone. The spoke in the wheel was the fact that he was sentenced to a night on the sofa with an enticing woman only a room away, and definitely inaccessible. Oh, it would be heaven itself to make love with Chapel Barclay. So much passion was lingering just below the surface, passion he was convinced she was not totally aware of.

Who was Chapel Barclay? he mused. And even more, did she really know who she was? How could she settle on her way of life, on being independent and needing no one, when she had nothing to compare it to? That was like saying she cared only for pecan pie when she'd never tasted pumpkin! Dumb simile, but it was true!

Why was he spending so much mental energy thinking about her? Ben wondered, his gaze still riveted on Chapel. The planes would probably be flying tomorrow, and he'd go home to Santa Fe and never see her again. Of course, he didn't *have* to leave immediately, as he'd left a whole stack of ready-to-go columns with Cappy at the paper. He'd been so edgy lately that he'd worked ahead in case he decided to take a vacation. Maybe he'd— What he should do was watch television and quit gawking at Chapel!

He settled into a more comfortable position,

directed his attention to the television, and only then realized he was supposedly watching a documentary on the mating habits of the polar bear. He pushed himself to his feet and crossed the room, then flipped through the stations until he found a movie with a vaguely familiar actress crying her eyes out as a man stormed out the door.

"Whatever," Ben muttered, sinking back onto the sofa.

She really wished Ben would sit still! Chapel thought. She'd read the same paragraph four times and had no idea what it said. Ben was just so . . . there! People spent evenings like this every night of the week, but *she* never had! She'd simply never sat around in her living room trying to concentrate on her work with a vibrantly masculine man perched on the other end of the sofa! She was just so aware of him, so conscious of every move he made. Going out with men was one thing, but this was entirely different. It was . . . intimate. Oh, how dumb! The man was watching television, for Pete's sake!

Chapel turned back to her work, but the television destroyed her concentration. She found herself listening to the dialogue.

"So, you've come back," the woman was saying. "What's wrong? Was your mistress busy?"

"I'm not sleeping with her!" the man said.

"Do you actually expect me to believe that?" she demanded.

"Don't buy it, honey," Ben said. "He's guilty as sin. Throw the bum out!"

Chapel peered at the television with one eye, then looked at the file again.

"Oh, Angelica María, I love only you," the man said.

Chapel peeked again and saw the man haul the woman into his arms and plaster kisses all over her face.

"Oh, Federico, my beloved," Angelica María said, adhering herself to his body. "Love me! Take me to your bed! Make me yours for eternity!"

"Boo-hiss!" Ben said. "The guy's conning you, lady. It was the mistress's bridge night, that's all."

"He seems sincere," Chapel said.

"Oh, bull," Ben said. "He's after her money."

"Angelica María, you are all I need," Federico said, lifting her into his arms.

"Just you and your checkbook, Angie," Ben said. "He's been to the racetrack again. The loan sharks are after him."

"But look at his face," Chapel said. "He's . . . he's caressing her with his eyes."

"He's what?" Ben said, bursting into laughter. "His hands are pretty busy too. She's a goner, poor kid. He'll jump on her body, then hit her up for ten grand. Angie baby needs a keeper."

"She does not!" Chapel said. "She knows her own mind. She won't allow Fred to use her like that. She realizes he has weaknesses, but he sincerely loves her. He—they're in the bedroom? What channel is this?"

"Beats me," Ben said, lifting one shoulder in a shrug. "Think this is a dirty flick? Ho-ho! Look at that! Will you look at that!"

Both Chapel and Ben were absorbed in the melodrama. Half an hour passed, then Ben burst out, "He tells her he's going to go lock the front door and—"

"That rat!" Chapel yelled. "He took all the money out of her purse! What a sorry son-of-a-gun! We'll sue!" She laughed. "I'll get him five-to-ten for petty theft or something."

"He stole her virtue and her money!" Ben said, getting up and turning off the television. "That is the worst movie I've ever seen. He does a nice job of dying, though, when the hoods gun him down for not paying his debts."

"How do you know?"

"I've already seen it."

"You cheater. You knew Fred was a louse," Chapel said, unable to control her laughter. "I thought he was a nice guy until he ripped off her money. Oh, well, what do I know?"

"Just goes to show you that first impressions can be wrong," Ben said, suddenly serious as he sat back down on the sofa. "You'd made up your mind that I was a sexist, remember?"

"Well, I . . ."

"And now, Chapel?" he went on, his voice low. "Do you still believe I'm out to exploit men and women, turn them into nothing more than sex objects?"

"A lot of what you've said about the advice in your column is confusing. I just don't know what to think. You mention communication, talking and sharing, but you don't seem to place very much emphasis on it. To me they're the key, the foundation of a relationship, not empty gestures of red bows and bubble baths. I do know, though, that if a woman wants to be treated as an equal in the professional world, she has to downplay her feminine attributes."

"Nope," he said, shaking his head. "Wrong."

"Ben, I'm out there every day! I'm very aware of how it goes."

"I realize that you have to dress in a certain style to present an image of intelligence and respectability. But you don't have to submerge your femininity completely. For instance, you could have worn a bright scarf with that gray suit on the telecast, and looked both professional and womanly."

"You've got an awful lot to say about something you know absolutely nothing about!" she said, jumping to her feet and dumping the files onto the floor. "You're full of hot air, Dear Ben!"

"Dammit," he said, getting up and gripping her by the arms. "You're a stubborn woman, Chapel Barclay. You've made up your mind about how things are, and you won't even consider the possibility that you could be wrong. Do you like it in your narrow little existence? It's safe in there, right? If you don't test out your femininity, no one can say it's lacking."

"Shut up!" she said, sudden tears clinging to her lashes. "You're being despicable again!"

"Ah, hell, I made you cry."

"I am not crying," she said, as a tear slid down her cheek. "I never cry."

"Chapel, I'm sorry. I'm so very sorry I made you cry."

A sob caught in her throat as his mouth melted over hers. She never cried, she thought frantically. And yet she was crying, and she didn't know why. And Ben was kissing her, and she should demand that he stop, but she didn't want to. Oh, dear heaven, she didn't want to! She felt so good, so right in his arms. Alive and whole and, yes, so very glad she was a woman.

He gathered her close to his chest, his tongue exploring each sweet, hidden corner of her mouth. Flames of desire licked through her, leaving her trembling as she sank against his strong body. His arousal pressed against her, a bold announcement of his desire for her. She burrowed her fingers into his silky hair to bring him closer yet.

"Chapel," he gasped, tearing his mouth from hers.

"Ben," she said, her voice a serene whisper.

"Damn." He gently pushed her away from him. "I want you so much and— Damn," he said again, raking an unsteady hand through his hair.

Chapel blinked her eyes once slowly as she drifted out of her mindless daze.

"Ben, I . . ." she began, then took a deep breath. "I . . . have never felt so . . . I mean, when you kiss me something very strange happens that . . . Oh, my."

"Tell me about it," he said, his voice gritty. "I'm not in terrific shape here myself. You are one very passionate, very desirable woman, Chapel Barclay."

"Me? I am?" She smiled. "I'll be darned. No one ever said that to me before. Of course, I've never been kissed quite like that before, either. I guess you have . . . uh, a lot of experience."

"Don't dump this on me! You did your part! We shared that kiss, lady!"

"Well, don't get all in a huff! I accept my responsibility as a willing participant in an equally gratifying . . . exchange."

"Oh, good. Super," he said, glaring at her. "Toss a little lawyer jargon around. That won't erase the fact that I want to make love to you! How do you feel about that kind of exchange, counselor?"

"No," she said, folding her arms across her chest.

"No? Just no? Don't you want to spiel out a fifteen-minute dissertation?"

"No."

"Well, hell! I've been turned down before, but never quite so . . . You're supposed to list the reasons, Chapel. Stuff like we hardly know each other, this is all happening too quickly, junk like that. A cold, flat 'no' is rough on a man's ego."

"Oh. Well, we hardly know each other, and it's all happening too quickly. There, how's that?"

"I don't believe you," he said, squinting at her. "What's the real reason you won't make love with me?"

"Well," she said with a sigh, "it's very simple. I won't, because I want to."

"Huh?"

"You're doing tricky things to my mind and body, and I don't understand what it all means. I want to make love with you, am a breath away from doing exactly that, which means I've lost control of myself, and I can't deal with that. I alone am responsible for my actions, and I have no intention of succumbing to something I can't comprehend."

"What chapter in the feminist handbook is that in?"

"Oh, stuff it!" she said, and sat down on the sofa.

"I could seduce you, you know," he said, waggling a long finger at her.

"Don't be silly. You, the great advocator of

romance, would resort to seduction in its purest form?"

"No," he said, slouching onto the sofa, "I'd hate myself. I've never taken a woman to bed who wasn't perfectly aware of what she was doing. Chapel, you are an extremely intelligent woman. Don't you think if you put your superbrain into action, you could figure out all the things you don't understand about what's happening between us?"

"I'm not sure. In the meantime . . ."

"Yeah?" he said, sitting bolt upright. "In the meantime . . . ?"

"Would you like some hot chocolate?"

Four

An expression of shock crossed Ben's face, then he laughed.

"Yes," he said, grinning at Chapel, "I'd like some hot chocolate. Do you have any marshmallows?"

"Oh, my, yes," she said, heading toward the kitchen. "One cannot have hot chocolate without marshmallows, can one? Certainly not."

"Yep," Ben said quietly, still smiling, "she's really something." He jumped to his feet. "I'd better offer to help, or I'll end up being despicable again."

Chapel absently stirred the milk in the pan as a jumble of voices echoed in her mind. What she had said to Ben was true. She wanted to make love with him, and therefore she couldn't. She couldn't because she didn't understand the new, strange power he had over her body and her sense of reasoning. When he kissed her, she ached for more. She wanted the fulfillment his masculinity promised.

She was no longer the child taken under the wing of the older professor who had treated her gently as he led her into the world of lovemaking. She had gone to him willingly, cherished his words of endearment, yet in some dusty corner of her mind had continually wondered if there shouldn't be more, a greater intensity of feeling when they became one. Sex had been pleasant, but certainly not enough to make a fuss over.

But somehow she knew with Ben it would be different. His touch alone ignited passions she'd never felt before. She instinctively knew that if she made love with Ben, he would consume her—body, soul, and mind. And what of her heart? What if in the midst of the tangle of confusion she fell in love with him?

"No," she said aloud, shaking her head.

"Always talk to hot chocolate?" Ben asked, coming up beside her.

"What? Oh, I was just thinking."

"Need some help with the chocolate?"

"No, it's all ready."

She scooped the hot chocolate mix into two mugs and poured in the steaming milk. Then she set the mugs on a tray, along with a bag of marshmallows and a plate of cookies. She reached for the tray at the same moment Ben did, and his large hands covered hers. She stared at his hands, so dark against her pale skin, and felt the warmth of his body envelop her. She slowly lifted her gaze to his, knowing he was looking at her, knowing she would once again drown in the depths of his dark eyes.

"Ben, don't," she whispered.

"Don't what, Chapel?" he asked, his voice low. "Don't look at you? Don't desire you? Don't want to make love to you? What's happening between us can't be found in one of your textbooks with a precise, logical explanation as to why. Yes, I want you physically, but it's more than that. There's so much inside of you—buried, forgotten, or never known. I want to know the real Chapel Barclay that I've only had a glimpse of, the one with purple feet and laughter like sunshine. Open those inner doors, for yourself, and for me. Give us a chance."

"No," she said, starting to pull her hands free.

"Yes." He tightened his hold. "Something happened the minute I met you. I couldn't get you off my mind and was sincerely concerned that you were upset by what had happened on that television show. Some people might say I was an idiot to come clear across town in this weather to check on you. But I had no choice, don't you see? You were there in my thoughts, haunting me, calling to me. And what did I find? An uptight spinster who tossed me back out into the snow? No. Oh, no. I discovered Chapel Barclay, the woman, who has depths that she herself is not totally aware of."

"Ben, please."

"You've done extraordinary things with your career, your intelligence. But you skipped over living, loving. Don't you want to build snowmen? See flowers bloom in the spring? Don't you want to discover who you really are?"

"I know exactly who I am!"

"Do you?" He asked the question so softly, she barely heard him.

"Why are you doing this?" she asked, her voice trembling. "What am I, some kind of interesting project? Let's see what makes a superbrain tick? Or is it just your male ego? The fact that I publicly denounced the great Dear Ben and his syrupy, sexist advice column? Whichever it is, I won't play this game with you!"

Ben's jaw tightened and he lifted his hands from hers. Anger flashed through his dark eyes, then something else that Chapel could neither recognize, nor put a name to. Tension crackled in the air as they stood staring at each other, then Ben finally shook his head and took a step backward.

"Those drinks are getting cold," he said quietly. "Shall I carry the tray?"

"No, thank you," she said, picking it up and brushing past him.

He turned to follow her, then stopped as his gaze swept over the table. The two paper napkin flowers were still there, set side by side in the center.

"Okay, darlin'," he said under his breath. "We'll just take this slow and easy." Oh, really? he asked himself. He was supposed to get on a plane tomorrow and leave this arctic zone. He was going home to—to what? The restlessness, this nameless yearning, would follow him back to Santa Fe. Had Chapel's accusation been closer to the truth than he realized? Did he see her as a challenge of sorts, a puzzle to be solved to liven up his suddenly empty existence? That, maybe, he could understand. But, no, it wasn't anything remotely close to idle curiosity. It was Chapel herself, and he knew it.

She was weaving a silken web around him, pulling him closer to her with her green eyes and cinnamon-colored hair, her fiery temper and wind-chime laughter. The desire within him went beyond his own physical needs. He wanted to give her pleasure, teach her the ecstasy of true sharing, of becoming one with another person. There was no way in hell he was going to leave Detroit tomorrow!

"Ben?" Chapel called. "Don't you want your chocolate?"

"What? Oh, sure." He walked into the living room and joined her on the sofa.

"Is it still hot enough?" she asked.

"It's fine," he said, dropping a marshmallow into the mug.

"We certainly argue a lot, don't we?" she said quietly.

"No, we . . . express our opinions. Chapel, I think it's only fair to tell you that even if the planes are flying tomorrow, I'm not going back to Santa Fe."

"Why not?"

"I have some vacation time coming, and I'm going to take it because I want to get to know you better, and I can't do that if I'm halfway across the country. And, no, you are not some kind of fascinating project. You're a fascinating woman, and there's a helluva big difference between the two. I meant it when I said something happened when I met you. I intend to find out what that something is."

"Did it ever occur to you that I might have a say in this?" she asked, her green eyes flashing. "Just because *you've* decided to, quote, 'get to know me better,' doesn't mean I'm interested in seeing *you* again, Ben Simmons! You're taking an awful lot for granted here."

"Mind if I take a shower?"

"What?"

"Some of my muscles ache from trudging through that wind and snow. A good hot shower would fix me right up. Then I think I'll turn in. It's been a long day."

Chapel set her mug on the tray with a thud and glared at Ben. He smiled at her engagingly, and she stomped into the bedroom.

"I'll get you some towels," she said over her shoulder.

"You're most kind. You run a classy hotel here."

"You're pushing me, Simmons!" she yelled.

Ben chuckled in delight.

A few minutes later Chapel returned with a blanket, a pillow, towels, a new toothbrush, and a razor, all of which she dumped unceremoniously onto the sofa.

"Bathroom is in there," she said. "I'll wait here until you're finished."

"Yes, ma'am," he said. "Whatever you say, ma'am. Oh, don't feel that you have to make up my bed. You're not the maid around here, you know."

"Go!" she said, pointing to the bedroom.

After he disappeared, Chapel sank onto the sofa. Ben wasn't returning to Santa Fe tomorrow, she thought. He was staying in Detroit. Because of her.

That was crazy! Why would he do such a cuckoo thing? She told him once an hour that he was despicable. She'd made it very clear that his column should be banned. Banned, for crying out loud. What did he mean by "I want to get to know you better"? Well, she had a newsflash for Sexy Simmons: She never intended to see him again!

Never see him again? she asked herself. Not ever? Never share another one of those incredible kisses, never again be held in those strong arms? That was rather . . . depressing. But it was for the best, Chapel decided. Ben confused her. Not only did he make her body go wild when he touched her, but he continually questioned the way she lived her life. He placed such emphasis on building snowmen, and seeing flowers bloom in the spring. She had no room for such nonsense in her world.

She picked up the tray and carried it into the kitchen. After setting it on the counter, she absently ran her fingertip around the edge of one of the mugs. Flowers in the spring, she mused. Ben wasn't just talking about flowers. He was referring to a way of life that encompassed far more than a successful career. Had she been so intent on accomplishing her intellectual goals that she'd lost track of herself, of her own inner needs?

With a deep frown on her face Chapel rinsed out the mugs, put the cookies back in the canister, and replaced the bag of marshmallows in the cupboard. Her gaze fell on the paper flowers on the table, and she picked them up, cradling them in her hands. As she moved to throw them in the trash, she hesitated, then with a defeated sigh put them back on the table.

"He's turning my brain into scrambled eggs," she muttered. "I really wish he'd go back to his cactus."

She returned to the living room and collected her files and pad from the floor, placing them in her briefcase.

"Bathroom is all yours," Ben said suddenly from behind her, causing her to jump.

She turned and her breath caught in her throat. He was clad only in his jeans, which rode low on his narrow hips. He was vigorously drying his hair with a towel, and she could see the powerful muscles in his arms and chest flexing. His tanned chest was covered by moist, tawny hair that disappeared below the waistband of his jeans. She caught the faint aroma of soap along with a scent that shouted "male," and swallowed heavily as her heart beat a wild cadence.

He was without a doubt the most intimidatingly masculine man she had ever seen, she thought. Ben Simmons was incredible. Just absolutely beautiful. But! He was flaunting that scrumptious body in front of her on purpose! He knew he was gorgeous, and he was trying to jar her, to weaken her resistance. Oh, how very clever of Mr. Simmons, but it wasn't going to work! He wasn't dealing with a dunderhead here!

"I put my coat over the hamper," he said. "Okay?"

"Sure," she said, waving a hand breezily. Had her voice squeaked? No, it sounded fine. Didn't it? Oh, Lord, she had to get out of this room! "Well, good night," she said, starting to move past him. "I hope you'll be warm enough."

"And if I get cold?" he asked, his voice low and rumbly. "What then?"

The man just didn't quit! she thought, as the familiar tingle danced up her spine. "Then put your clothes back on!" she yelled.

"Why are you hollering again?" he asked, an expression of pure innocence on his face. "That was a reasonable question from a man who isn't accustomed to this weather. I just thought there might be some . . . uh, exercises I should do to keep the blood moving through my veins. No, huh?"

"No! Just wrap up in your snuggy blanket."

"Got it," he said, nodding solemnly. "I just hope I don't freeze to death. You'll have a tough time explaining my corpse to the cops."

"I'll risk it. Good night."

"Chapel, wait," he said quietly, placing his hands on her shoulders. "I really do want to get to know you better. It's important to me that you believe that it's not because I see you as a freaky challenge or something. You're a beautiful, desirable, intriguing woman. Intelligent, too, of course. I know you don't like me a helluva lot, and probably don't trust me at all, but will you give me a chance to prove I'm sincere?"

"Oh, Ben," she said, sighing deeply, "I don't know. You confuse me."

"That's good, don't you see? You confuse me, too, because something is happening here that I don't understand. Your confusion means that you're aware of it too. The difference is I want to find out what it is, and you're on the brink of running away from it. Don't run from me, Chapel," he said, slowly lowering his head to hers. "I won't hurt you. I would never hurt you."

Don't kiss this man! Chapel's mind screamed, as

Ben slid his tongue seductively over her lower lip. Do it! her body countered. Her body won the battle.

She slid her hands up his chest, tangling her fingers in the enticing, tawny curls. He gathered her close as his tongue delved deep into her mouth. The masculine scent of his skin was intoxicating, and she wrapped her arms around his neck and pressed against him. Heartbeats quickened and breathing became labored, as the kiss grew urgent, frenzied. His hands skimmed over her hips to cup her buttocks and fit her against him. The soft purr from Chapel's throat was matched by Ben's groan, then he lifted his head and drew a ragged breath.

"Oh, Chapel," he said, his voice raspy, "what you do to me is unbelievable. I touch you and— What am I going to do about you?"

"Do?" Her own voice was unsteady as she drew a trembling breath.

"Yes, do! I just stood here asking you to give me a chance to prove I'm sincere, that I won't hurt you in any way. Then I kiss you, and all I can think about is making love with you. I'm no better than Federico!"

"Oh, for heaven's sake," she said, bursting into laughter. "I doubt seriously that you plan to steal my money."

"Now you're laughing again," he said, his brows knitted in a frown. "I need a scorecard to keep up with you."

"We intellects have been known to be moody, strange, even borderline weird. You should catch the first plane available and flee," she said, smiling at him brightly.

"You don't scare me." He brushed his lips quickly over hers. "Good night."

But he scared her, she thought. "Good night, Ben," she said. "Sleep well."

Sleep well? he thought, as Chapel closed the bedroom door behind her. Fat chance. He needed to go jogging or swimming to work off the knot in his gut, the physical frustration that had him strung out. Never in his entire life had he desired a woman the way he did Chapel Barclay!

Forget it, he told himself, flopping down on the sofa and shutting off the light. Don't think about her. Do not think, Simmons! Holy cow, it's freezing in here!

In her dream Chapel was being crushed by a mountain of marshmallows. They held her pinned in place, unable to move, and when she struggled against the weight, she was incapable of freeing herself. She forced herself to wake up, blinking in the darkness. In the next instant she stiffened in horror. The marshmallows were real! She couldn't move!

"Mmm," the marshmallows mumbled.

Her hand shot out and thudded against a warm, bare chest. Reality crept into her consciousness, and she became aware that a bare leg was slung across both of hers, her flannel nightgown was twisted around her thighs, and a muscular arm was beneath her breasts. Ben!

"Ben Simmons!" she shrieked. "You rotten reprobate, get out of my bed!"

"What? What?" he said, sitting bolt upright and dragging the blankets with him.

"Oh-h-h, you're despicable!"

"Huh?"

"You've got two seconds to—"

"Chapel?" he said, shaking his head to clear the fogginess.

"Who do you think it is, you sleazeball? How dare you sneak in here and glom all over me like a marshmallow!"

"I was freezing to death! My teeth were chattering! My toes were numb again! I didn't glom, I just very politely took half of the bed."

"Oh, ha! You glommed!"

"I must have moved after I fell asleep. That's instincts of survival. My subconscious went in search of body heat. Get it?"

"The only getting to be got is you getting out of this bed!"

"What?"

"Go!"

"Oh, Chapel, have a heart. It's so damn cold out there. I'm just a good ol' boy from the Sunny West. I'm not used to this iceberg weather. I won't touch you, I swear! I'll stay so close to the edge, I'll have to hang on by my fingertips. Please?"

"Shh, I'm thinking," she said. "I have to sort this through."

"Take all the time you need," he said, burrowing beneath the blankets.

Now what? Chapel wondered. There was a man in her bed, for crying out loud. To be more precise Benjamin Simmons was in her bed! This would never do.

Well, she could see where he could have gotten cold, as she only had one spare blanket, and he wasn't accustomed to these kinds of temperatures. But still, he had no right to just crawl into her bed. But then again, wouldn't it be all right if he solemnly swore to stay on his side of the bed? Could she trust him? Yes, she could. He'd already said he'd never seduce her into doing something she hadn't intended to do. Okay, she'd figured it all out.

"Ben?"

Silence.

"Ben?" she said, sitting up and peering at the lump of blankets. "He went back to sleep!" Well, thanks a whole helluva lot! she fumed, flopping back onto the pillow and yanking up the covers. That certainly didn't say much for her irresistible, voluptuous self! The man had just rolled over and conked out. "You don't do much for a person's ego, Simmons," she muttered, closing her eyes.

On the other side of the bed, the lump under the blankets was smiling.

Years of conditioning are not undone by a change in environment. Hours later when the alarm sounded, Chapel reached out her hand and shut it off. Ben reached out his hand and firmly grasped Chapel's breast.

"Aaak!" she screamed.

"What? What?" Ben mumbled, his hand still firmly in place.

"Move your big paw!"

"Oh, this one?" he asked, his thumb beginning a

rhythmic motion across the soft flannel. He rolled onto his side and rested on his arm as he gazed down at her. Her nipple grew taut beneath his foray, and he heard her sharp intake of breath. "So warm, so soft," he said, his voice husky with sleep. "You're nice to wake up to, Chapel."

"Ben . . ."

"Very nice," he added, and kissed her.

Good morning, Ben Simmons, she thought dreamily, as she circled his neck with her arms.

The kiss was slow and sensuous, and took her breath away. His hand slid down to the flat plane of her stomach and rested there, creating a circle of heat that penetrated her body and swept through her like a raging fire. He shifted his weight, one leg pinning both of hers as he moved her partially beneath him. Their tongues dueled in a seductive dance that was matched by the pulsating sensation in the secret core of Chapel's femininity.

He lifted his head to draw a ragged breath, then claimed her mouth again. Her hands slid beneath his arms to splay over his back, and he trembled slightly under her feathery touch. His manhood pressed against her in a bold announcement of his need of her, and she felt gloriously alive.

Oh, how she wanted this man to make love to her, she thought. His body held such a magnificent promise of fulfillment, such power and strength. She ached with a wondrous new yearning. And here in her arms was the man who would unravel the mysteries of her femininity, take her to a place she had never truly been.

"Chapel," Ben gasped, starting to pull away.

"No, don't go," she said breathlessly. "Make love to me, Ben. Please. I do want you so much."

He clenched his jaw and closed his eyes, striving for control. He had to think! This was Chapel, and she was offering herself to him. God, he wanted her. But had he run roughshod over her reasoning, heightened her passion to a point where she was no longer thinking straight? Once he had started kissing her, he'd been unable to stop. He'd drowned in the taste, the feel of her. But what if she hated him afterward? He didn't know what to do!

"Ben?" she said, her voice trembling slightly. "Don't you want me?"

A moan rumbled up from his chest, and he brought his mouth down hard onto hers in a punishing kiss. In the next instant he rolled onto his back, flinging his arm over his eyes, his breathing labored and raspy.

"I have never," he muttered, "been so mentally screwed up in my life! I want to make love to you so much. Chapel, don't start in on a spiel about being an independent, liberated woman in charge of her own body, destiny, and all that nonsense, because in your case it's a bunch of bull!"

"Well, I never!" she snapped, folding her arms over her breasts.

"I know that!"

"Huh?"

"You never sleep around, dammit!" he roared, sitting up. "You'll hate me. You'll throw me out in the snow to freeze my buns off! Chapel," he said, his voice gentling, "I don't know what to do. If we make love and you regret it, I couldn't handle it. You're too

important to me, don't you see? I have to be sure that
you're sure, and I don't know how to be sure that
you're sure. Ah, hell, I'm blithering like an idiot. Do
you understand what I'm saying to you? If you do,
would you mind explaining it to me, because my
brain is mush. Please don't ask me the condition of
my body. I'm a dying man!"

Chapel smiled as a tender warmth filled her. She
lifted her hand and placed it on Ben's cheek, feeling
the stubble of his beard beneath her palm. She had
never felt so cherished as she did at that moment.
Somewhere in the back of her mind she knew she
should be insulted by Ben's accusation that she was
not a liberated woman. But it was only a flicker of a
thought, for first and foremost was the realization
that she might slowly, but surely, be falling in love
with Benjamin Simmons.

"Quit looking at me like that," he said hoarsely. "I
see serenity in your eyes, and trust. Do you trust me,
Chapel?"

"Yes," she said softly.

"But to do what? Be what? A good lover because I
have muscles in all the right places? It has to mean
more than that. It's never mattered to me before, but
with you it does. I have to know you're going to give
us a chance to really discover what's happening
between us. Dammit, Chapel, I won't be a one-night
stand! Good Lord, this is all the stuff *you're* supposed
to be saying!"

A tiny bubble of laughter escaped from Chapel's
lips.

"That's it! I've had it!" Ben said, turning around to

sit on the edge of the bed. "I'm getting out of this bed!
I'm—"

"You are," she interrupted, trailing her fingertip
over the steely muscles in his back, "the dearest,
sweetest, most wonderful man I have ever met. You
confuse me, and frighten me, and make me rejoice in
the fact that I'm a woman. You make me want to build
snowmen, and see the flowers in the spring. I would
never regret making love with you, Ben, because I
know exactly what I'm doing. Yes, there is something
happening between us, and we owe it to ourselves to
find out what it is."

He turned his head to look at her over his shoulder,
and their eyes met in a gaze that was open and
revealing. There was a sharper awareness between
them, a greater understanding. There was trust and
tenderness and warmth. And there was desire.
Silken threads of sensuality drew them closer, closer,
until Chapel lifted her arms and welcomed Ben into
her embrace.

He stretched out next to her, gathering her to his
chest. Then he held her, simply held her, as he buried
his face in the fragrant cloud of her hair. He felt a
tightening in his throat as a sense of possessiveness
toward Chapel swept over him. And there was more.
The void within him that had beleaguered him for the
past weeks began to change from a chilling darkness
to a sunny warmth, like a field of wildflowers in the
spring. Chapel was filling him, making him whole
once again.

"Thank you," he said, not realizing he had spoken
out loud.

She moved her head back to look at him as she

heard the tremor in his voice. "Is something wrong?" she asked.

"Oh, no, no, not at all," he said, smiling at her warmly. "Everything is fine, better than it's been in a long, long time."

And then he kissed her.

Five

Ben kissed Chapel's lips, her cheeks, the tip of her nose. The slender column of her throat received serious loving attention, then he claimed her mouth again, delving his tongue into the inner darkness.

His hand covered her stomach, and she became acutely aware of her ridiculous red flannel nightgown. Even though Ben was kissing her, a rush of tormenting thoughts assaulted her. Ben was no doubt used to worldly, sophisticated women, who knew all about pleasing a man. She was a dud, a know-nothing in a granny gown! She was a top-notch lawyer, but what did she know about being a woman? Chapel asked herself. Not a whole helluva lot!

"Chapel?" Ben said. "You've tensed up. Are you frightened?"

"It could be worse, I suppose."

"What?"

"Last year I had a pair of those jammies with the feet, like baby's sleepers."

"That's nice," he said, appearing rather confused.

"Look at this nightgown!"

"It's red?"

"How can you make love to a woman in a red flannel nightgown? I look like a thermometer."

He chuckled deep in his throat. "You look like a Christmas present, and I'm going to unwrap you."

"Oh, Ben, I wish I was more experienced."

"Do you think I expect you to perform for me, Chapel?" he asked, a muscle in his jaw twitching slightly. "The fact that you haven't been around the block is refreshing, unique, rare. I also think your nightgown is the cutest thing I've ever seen. It's right up there with your fuzzy purple slippers. We're going to make love, Chapel. Together. It's going to be wonderful."

"Oh, Ben," she whispered, circling his neck with her arms. Was she really falling in love with this man? Would she even know it if she were? Her feelings for him were so strange, almost frightening in their intensity. Was this love?

"Chapel," he murmured, then lowered his mouth to hers.

Delicious sensations swirled through Chapel, and she welcomed them. Ben's tongue dipped and dueled with hers in a seductive dance, and a purr escaped from her throat. His heat invaded her body, and she voiced no objection when he threw back the blankets, swept her nightgown up over her head, and dropped it on the floor. The cool air tingled against her skin, and her nipples grew taut.

"Oh, Chapel," he said, his voice vibrant with passion, "you're beautiful, like ivory velvet. Beautiful."

She gasped with pleasure as he drew the bud of her breast into his mouth. She cupped his head in her hands to press him closer to her throbbing flesh. A liquid warmth began in the core of her femininity and spread throughout her. As he turned his attention to her other breast, his hand roamed in lazy circles over her stomach to her thighs. He parted her legs and found her ready for him, and she shifted restlessly beneath the sweet torture of his foray. His arousal was hard against her, filled with the promise of what would be hers.

The knot of need tightened within Ben as he held himself back, trembling with desire. His body ached for release, but his mind fiercely demanded he take it slowly. It had to be perfect for Chapel. Perfect! She was trusting him with more than just her body, and he knew that. She was trusting him to release the woman locked deep inside her. And, dear Lord, he was scared to death! What if he failed her?

"Chapel," he said, his voice strained.

"Oh, please," she said, gripping his shoulders. "I want you so much."

He moved away only long enough to rid himself of

his underwear, then lay beside her again, leaning on one arm as he stroked her cheek with his other hand.

"I want—no, *need*—this to be perfect for you," he said.

"It will be. Come to me, Ben."

"Soon."

His hand trailed a heated path over her slender form, touching, caressing, stroking her passion into a raging flame. Where his hands had gone, his lips followed, until she was writhing with desire, tossing her head restlessly on the pillow. His muscles shuddered from the effort of his control, and a sheen of moisture glistened on his tanned skin. But still he held back, delaying the moment of ecstasy when he would bury himself deep within Chapel's honeyed warmth.

"Ben! Please!" she cried, a sob catching in her throat.

He moved over her in answer to her plea, hesitating above her as he searched her flushed face.

"Yes," she whispered. "Oh, yes."

In one smooth, powerful motion he filled her, consumed her, claimed her as his. She closed her eyes to savor the magnificent sensations coursing through her. Ben held still, watching the wondrous expressions flicker across her face. Slowly she lifted her lashes and smiled a gentle smile, a trusting smile, that made his breath catch.

The ancient dance of lovers began. With steady, rhythmic thrusts Ben moved within her. She clutched his shoulders and matched his movements as they grew stronger, more intense. He slid his arm beneath her hips to lift her to him, and she moaned in pleasure. Higher they soared. She arched her back to bring him closer yet, as she sought a treasure that had no name. A mysterious yearning for something she did not understand churned within her. But it had to be hers, this elusive gift her body was straining to find. And then at last with a crashing crescendo she was there.

"Ben!"

"Yes," he moaned. "Don't be afraid. I'm here."

Ecstasy rocketed through her and she dug her fingers into his shoulders. She was swept away in a maelstrom of glorious sensations, then heard Ben call her name as he shuddered above her. He collapsed against her, his strength spent, then pushed himself up to rest on trembling arms.

"Chapel?" he asked, his voice shaky. "Oh, darlin', please, talk to me. Tell me you're all right. Tell me it was—"

"Wonderful," she said, smiling at him as she cupped his face in her hands. "I have never . . . I didn't know . . . Oh, Ben, there just aren't words to tell you how I feel."

"Thank God," he said, burying his face in her hair.

She ran her hands over the moist skin of his muscular back and smiled. She had come alive under Ben's kiss and touch, and her body was singing with sensual joy. Was this love? Ben had just called her darlin', and she hadn't thrown a fit. That had to mean something! But in the next instant she wondered about that. Did she want to be in love? Even more, had she chosen wisely?

"You are something," Ben said, brushing his lips over hers. He moved gently away, then nestled her close to his side. "You're so trusting and giving, Chapel. You made me feel ten feet tall. You're not sorry we made love, are you?"

"No, no, of course not. It was beautiful. I'm not going to accuse you of seducing me to the point that I didn't know what I was doing. Making love with you was a rational, logical decision on my part. I accept equal responsibility for my participation in what took place. Would you hand me my nightgown, please? I want to check on the weather."

"What? Oh, sure." He reached to the floor for the red flannel gown. "Here."

"Thank you," she said. She slipped the gown over her head and scooted off the bed.

Ben watched her leave the room, then flung his arm across his eyes. Rational? Logical? he thought. Dammit, she made it sound like a math equation. They'd made love, for Pete's sake, not solved a trigonometry problem! And it hadn't been just physical either! There had been emotions involved, emotions he'd never felt before. He had wanted to give maximum pleasure, answer her needs before his own, protect her. But maybe to Chapel it had been only "an equally gratifying exchange," as she was so fond of saying. Had he been nothing more than a body to her, a nice set of muscles, beef on the hoof? How dare she use him like that!

"The phone is working," Chapel said, breezing into the room, "the snow has stopped, and the streets are clear. I'll shower first."

"Whatever," he muttered, his arm still over his eyes.

Chapel studied Ben for a moment, wondering at

the surly tone of his voice, then gathered up her clothes and went into the bathroom. Closing the door behind her, she leaned against it and drew an unsteady breath.

Had she handled that right? she asked herself. She'd tried to appear worldly, sophisticated . . . liberated, for heaven's sake. She'd acknowledged her willing participation in their lovemaking, and tossed in the phrase *rational, logical decision* for good measure. The truth of the matter was, she was a wreck, a basket case. She didn't know whether to laugh or cry. She was a breath away from falling in love with Benjamin Simmons, and she was terrified.

"Who are you?" she asked her reflection in the mirror. Lord, she was confused. Every theory she'd based her life on was suddenly teetering. She was questioning for the first time the lessons learned at her mother's knee. *Independence, intelligence, career* were the key words. *Do it alone, or don't do it.* It had all stood her in good stead, brought her vast professional accomplishments. It had been her code of conduct. Until now. Until Ben.

She had to calm down, she told herself, stepping into the shower. She had to think this through. Ben was a temporary visitor to Detroit, and would soon be returning to Santa Fe. Whatever seed of caring for him that was growing within her had to be buried, forgotten. To fall in love with him would be a dreadful mistake. He would leave, and she would be alone. She'd always been alone, but this time, if she succumbed to the urges of her heart, it would be a chilling, empty loneliness. It mustn't happen! She was

Dr. Chapel Barclay, who needed no man to make her existence complete. Wasn't she?

She tilted her head back and let the water run over her. Her breasts still felt tender from Ben's love-making. His wonderful lovemaking. He had made her feel beautiful. Beautiful and womanly and cherished. She had the whimsical vision of strolling through rows and rows of lovely springtime flowers. With her hand held tightly in Ben's, she would drink in the heavenly fragrance of the delicate blossoms, then lift her smiling face to the sunshine, the blue sky, the fluffy white clouds.

"Oh, Ben," she whispered, "I'm so confused. And I'm suddenly so frightened."

After her shower she dressed and returned to the bedroom. Ben was still in bed.

"I'm finished with the bathroom," she said. "I'll make some coffee while you shower."

He pushed himself up and leaned against the head-board, crossing his arms over his bare chest as the blankets slid below his waist. His gaze swept over her dark, tailored suit, the tight bun at the nape of her neck. She picked an imaginary thread from her skirt.

"All ready for work, counselor?" he asked.

"Yes, and I'm late. I'll get the coffee going."

"Chapel," he said, his voice low, "come here."

"No, I . . ."

"Come here. Just for a minute."

She walked over to the bed, and with her hands clutched tightly together stared at a spot on the wall.

"Yes?" she said, her voice none too steady.

"Hey." He extracted one of her hands and cradling it in his two large ones. "What's wrong? Your eyes are huge and you look petrified. Talk to me. This is me. Ben."

"I know who you are," she said, shifting her gaze to him. "You're Dear Ben."

"Meaning?"

"When I looked out the window yesterday, I told you I felt as though we'd been lifted off to another planet. That was true in a way, but now we're back, and the world is out there again. I'm Dr. Chapel Barclay, attorney-at-law, and you are Ben Simmons, who dropped by Detroit for a brief stay and will be returning to Santa Fe and his column. A column—"

"That's speaks about romance, love, special times between two people. Don't try to use my column as a stumbling block between us, because it won't work. Surely you don't still believe that I advocate sexual exploitation, do you?"

"Oh, Ben," she said, her eyes suddenly filling with tears. "I don't know what I think about anything. My life was in order, I knew who I was. But now I'm so confused . . ."

"Listen to me," he said, pulling her down next to him. "Wonderful things are happening between us. Don't run, Chapel. Don't hide behind your walls, where you think it's safe. We'll figure it all out together, okay? No tears." He cupped her face in his hands and leaned toward her. "No tears for my Chapel."

Their mouths met softly, sensuously, and a wobbly sob escaped from Chapel. Ben slid his tongue between her lips, and she wrapped her arms around his neck as he gathered her close. Her entire body seemed flushed with desire, and her breasts grew heavy, aching for his touch. Their breathing sounded loud in the quiet room as the kiss became almost frantic.

Finally Ben pulled away and rested his forehead against Chapel's. "What you do to me is something else," he said in a hoarse voice. "I think you'd better go make that coffee."

"Yes, all right," she said breathlessly.

"But smile first," he said, tilting her chin up with his fingers. "Just a little?"

Their eyes met, and they both smiled. The passion that had flamed within them gradually cooled and was replaced by peacefulness.

So beautiful, Ben thought, trailing his thumb over the soft skin of Chapel's cheek. A delicate, fragile flower was Chapel Barclay. And he wanted to be there when she fully opened her petals. Would she let him stay close to her?

"The coffee," she said, and slowly stood and walked from the room.

With a sigh and a shake of his head Ben entered the bathroom and shut the door. After showering, he dressed, having collected his clothes from various locations. Chapel was setting cups of steaming coffee on the table when he entered the kitchen.

"I don't eat breakfast," she said. "You're welcome to fix yourself something if you're hungry."

"No, this is fine," he said, sitting down opposite her at the table.

"I imagine the planes are flying," she said, not looking at him.

"I'm not leaving today, Chapel. I told you that."

"Yes, I know, but I thought you might have changed your mind."

"Why?" he said sharply, smacking the table so hard with his palm that the coffee sloshed in the cups. "Because I slept with you and made my conquest, I might as well hit the road? Dammit, that's rotten!"

"I'm sorry! I can't presume to know what's going on in your head. As far as that goes, I can't figure out what's happening in my own head! I've got to get to work. One thing certainly stays consistent between us. We holler at each other every five seconds."

He chuckled softly. "Oh, we have other things we do rather well together too. For example, we . . ."

"Ben!" she said, blushing.

". . . make a great dinner as a team."

"Oh, Ben." She laughed. "I really must get to the office. Shall I drop you somewhere?"

"No, I'll call a taxi. I'd like to find that joker who dropped me in the middle of the snowdrift yesterday. No, forget that. He weighed about two thirty. Will you have dinner with me tonight?"

"Yes, that sounds very nice."

"Good. I'll pick you up at seven. I'll go phone for a cab."

A few minutes later they met at the door, both reaching for the knob at the same time. Their gazes met, then Ben raised his hands in a gesture of peace and stepped back to allow Chapel to open the door.

"Wait a minute," he said, pushing it closed again.

"What's wrong?"

"Nothing at all." He pulled her into his arms. "Not a thing."

The kiss was long and thorough, and Chapel was

trembling when Ben finally released her. With his arm tightly circling her shoulders they rode down in the elevator to the lobby.

"Your taxi is out front," Chapel said. "My car is in the underground garage. I'll see you tonight, Ben."

"Chapel, I— Okay, tonight." He smiled at her as he left the elevator. "Have a good day."

He watched as the elevator doors closed, then turned and walked slowly to the front of the building. The taxi was gone.

"Well, hell," he murmured, spinning on his heel and stalking back into the building. "Whatever happened to patience?"

Her office was empty when Chapel arrived, and she surmised that the side streets in Beth's subdivision had not yet been cleared of snow, delaying Beth's arrival at work. Chapel made the coffee, then settled in the soft leather chair behind her desk. Her gaze swept over the familiar surroundings, but she felt as though it had been a lifetime since she had been there.

So much had changed in the hours since she had entered the television studio to participate in *Opposite Views*. Her world had been turned topsy-turvy, and it was all due to Benjamin Simmons. The mere thought of him sent heated desire tingling throughout her, and the memories of their lovemaking echoed in her heart and mind.

If only she could separate the emotional from the physical, she mused. If only she could rejoice in the physical, cherish having made love with a magnificent man, and ignore the emotions that were inter-woven with all that had transpired with Ben. For with those emotions came the confusion and the fear.

Ben not only desired her body, but seemed to be seeking the path to her soul as well. Questions never before asked were pounding in Chapel's brain. Questions, she realized, that had to have answers. Was her world narrow, cold, and empty because she'd never allowed a man past her intellectual veneer? Had her determination to be accepted as a professional robbed her of the joys of her womanhood? Had she misconstrued the difference between romance and sexual exploitation? Was there a place in her life for building snowmen and strolling through the flowers in spring?

Was she falling in love with Ben Simmons?

With a sigh Chapel walked to the outer office and poured herself a cup of coffee. She listened to the messages on the answering machine, then flicked it off just as Beth bustled in the door.

"I have arrived!" Beth said. "I played toboggan in my car, but I'm here. Oh, that coffee smells yummy. Good morning, by the way."

"Hello," Chapel said, smiling. "Here. I'll even pour you a cup of my outstanding brew."

"Thank you," Beth said, as she hung up her coat.

"Did you have a nice evening?"

"Well, it was quiet. Frank was out in Livonia on a business call and simply couldn't make it home in the storm. He ended up in a motel for the night. He stumbled in this morning, and the poor dear looked so rumpled and tired. The crazy part was, I couldn't sleep last night without him next to me. I realized we'd never been apart, except when I was in the hospital having the babies. It was the strangest feeling to reach for him and find that he wasn't there."

"Did that—uh—bother you to realize you're so dependent on Frank?"

"Heavens no," Beth said, uncovering her typewriter. "It was good for me to realize how much I still love the old buzzard. I flung myself into his arms this morning like a young bride. After he recovered from the shock, he was pleased as punch. Bless his heart, he invited me out to dinner tonight. Isn't that . . . well . . ."

"Romantic?" Chapel suggested, frowning slightly.

"I realize that's not your favorite word after your encounter with Dear Ben on *Opposite Views*. But, yes, I'm looking forward to a very romantic evening with Frank, and it's long overdue. I'm afraid we've fallen into a rather drab routine, and it took last night to make me see that. Oops, there's the phone. Our day has begun."

"I'll be in my office," Chapel said, walking away. Darn it, she thought, sinking back into her chair. Now even Beth was all aglow over the prospect of a romantic evening. She'd never said much about her husband before, except that he was a good man. Then Ben comes to town and a romance epidemic starts, for crying out loud. Ridiculous. Dinner out was dinner out. She was sharing a meal with Ben, but she certainly didn't view it as some romantic interlude! Two people poked food in their mouths, chatted about various topics, and that was it. No big deal, right? Right! "So there," she muttered. Oh, great. She was doing her mature number again.

*   *   *

As Ben ate lunch in the hotel coffee shop he replayed in his mind the tape of *Opposite Views* he had watched on television in his room an hour before. He'd been cocky as hell, with his patronizing smiles and lazy drawl when he'd called Chapel 'darlin'. He'd interrupted her when she was speaking, and given the impression that he was snickering at everything she said. He was a louse! Chapel *had* been blitzed on that show, and it was all his fault. Well, he'd make it up to her. It was a wonder she hadn't decked him when he'd shown up at her door. But she'd let him in, and then it had begun, the filling of the emptiness within him with the essence of a beautiful, complicated, wondrous woman.

"She is something," he murmured, smiling.

"She must be, honey," the waitress said, pouring more coffee in his cup. "You're talking to yourself, and you've got a silly grin on your gorgeous face. I hope she loves you as much as you love her. Want some dessert?"

"What? Oh, no, thanks," Ben said. Was he in love with Chapel? Hell, he didn't know. He'd think about that later. And at seven that night he'd be with her.

Chapel sprayed a whiff of light cologne over her throat, then scrutinized her reflection in the full-length mirror. The soft wool dress was the exact shade of her eyes, nipped in at her waist, and fell in gentle folds to midcalf. She'd twisted her hair into a chignon after blow-drying it, then on an impulse had brushed it free to flow in gentle waves past her shoulders. And she was smiling.

It was reasonable, she assured herself, that she was looking forward to seeing Ben. He was, after all, a warm, attentive, handsome man, who made her feel alive and special. She simply wouldn't dwell on the confusion raging in her mind. She'd ignore her mental dilemma and enjoy Ben's company. And when he brought her home? What then? No, she wouldn't think about that now either.

"I'd make a great ostrich," she said merrily, placing her coat and purse on the sofa.

A knock sounded at the door, and with her smile still firmly in place, Chapel answered the summons.

Dressed in a beautifully tailored dark suit with a pale blue shirt and dark tie, Ben looked magnificent. Her heart immediately started beating wildly.

"Hello, Chapel," he said, his voice compellingly husky as he stepped into the room. "You look lovely."

"Thank you," she said, closing the door. "So do you. I mean, not lovely, but nice, handsome . . . oh, forget it," she said, throwing up her hands.

Ben chuckled and tossed his overcoat on the sofa, then drew her into the circle of his arms. "I need to kiss you," he said.

"You do?"

"Oh, yes, indeed. You don't mind, do you?"

"Not at all," she said, wrapping her arms around his neck.

And kiss her he did.

Ben kissed her until she was trembling in his arms. He kissed her until a strange roaring noise rushed in her ears, until his breathing was labored and raspy.

"Whew!" he said, when he finally released her. "I've been thinking about doing that all day. I went on a tour to watch them make cars, and I was day-dreaming about you. Right in the middle of nuts and bolts and hubcaps, you were on my mind."

Chapel laughed, then took a steadying breath. "I beat out that kind of competition?"

"Yep. Ready to go? I hope you're bringing a heavy coat. You would not believe how cold it is out there!"

"Do you have a taxi waiting?"

"I gave up on those guys. I rented a car, and have thoroughly studied a map of this gruesome town. Fear not, my dear, everything is under control."

Except Chapel Barclay, she thought, as they left the apartment. When she had opened the door and seen Ben, she had been filled with immeasurable joy. She had not wanted that kiss to end, but to continue right on into the bedroom. She had to settle down, get a grip on herself! She was behaving like an idiot. All they were doing was going out for dinner!

Ben had parked his car in the visitors' section of the underground garage, and he pulled Chapel close to his side as they walked across the echoing expanse.

"Ben, wait," she said, suddenly stopping. "Is it that bronze-colored car over there?"

"Yes."

"There's someone in it! Don't you see the outline of a head? It's a mugger!"

"No, it's not," he said, grinning at her. "That's your

surprise. I decided it would be more fun to let him ride along with us."

"My surprise? But it's not my birthday."

"Chapel," he said, turning her toward him by the shoulders, "it doesn't have to be your birthday to receive a surprise. Sometimes gifts are just to say, 'Hey, I was thinking about you.' In this case, that's partially true. The other reason is to apologize for my behavior on *Opposite Views*. I saw it this morning, and I'm not very proud of myself."

"You had a right to your opinion."

"That's true, but I didn't have to strut my stuff the way I did. I hope you'll forgive me."

"Oh, Ben, of course, I do. I was out of my element, and shouldn't have gone on that show in the first place."

"Then we'll chalk it up? Forget it?"

"Yes."

"Great," he said, kissing her quickly. "Now! Come meet the mugger in the backseat."

It was a teddy bear. An enormous pink and white teddy bear was smiling a mile-wide smile and staring straight ahead with huge, shiny black eyes. Chapel's hands flew to her cheeks, and a cry of delight escaped her lips. Ben hauled the bear out of the car and Chapel hugged it to her, tears misting her eyes as she gazed at Ben.

"Thank you," she said, her voice trembling. "I've never had anything like this. Never. It's a beautiful bear, a wonderful surprise. Oh, Ben, thank you so much."

"I'm glad you like it," he said. "I wasn't sure if you'd want it in your apartment, because I noticed you don't keep any knickknacks around. You should see my place. I have doodads everywhere. I guess a pink and white bear doesn't quite fit in. I'll understand if you give it to some kid."

"No! Oh, no, Ben! I adore it. It will have a place of honor. I don't have things like you're referring to because—because no one ever thought I'd want any, I guess."

"Not even your mother?" he asked gently.

"No. Ben, this is the nicest present I've ever received."

He nodded, then placed the bear carefully on the backseat. As he assisted Chapel into the car he was acutely aware of the lump in his throat.

The bear just smiled.

Six

The elegant restaurant the desk clerk at the hotel had recommended to Ben was one of the city's finest. Situated on the Detroit River, it offered a view of Canada. The mâitre d' led them to a candle lit table by the windows.

Chapel had liked the teddy bear, Ben thought, as he studied the wine list. Hell, she'd loved the thing. He'd bought it on an impulse, then nearly lost his nerve and left it at the hotel. The image of him presenting liberated Dr. Barclay, attorney-at-law, with a huge fuzzy pink-and-white bear had suddenly become ludicrous. But the bear had sat there grinning its fool head off, as if daring Ben to pick it up. So he'd grabbed it by the ear and hauled it out the door. And Chapel had lit up like a . . .

"Christmas tree," Ben said aloud.

"Pardon me?" Chapel asked.

"When are you going to put up your Christmas tree? The big day is less than two weeks away."

"I don't put up a tree. I have a holly berry centerpiece for the table, but that's it."

"Why?"

"Well, it's not as though I have children. I really don't make that big a fuss over Christmas, except for giving a few gifts."

"Grim," Ben said, shaking his head. "I think we should put up a tree in your living room."

"Don't be silly," she said, laughing softly.

"Well, it either goes there or in my hotel suite. Take your pick. You can vote. You women did earn the right to vote, you know. Providing, of course, you have the laundry finished before you go to the polls. So? Where do we put our tree?" Our tree? he thought. His and Chapel's? That sounded really good.

"You're serious, aren't you?" she said. Our tree? No, he hadn't meant it quite like that. Had he? No, of course not.

"Very serious," he said.

"How big of a tree?"

"I don't know. I'll wing it. Well?"

"I guess a small tabletop kind would be all right. I don't have any decorations though."

"I'll get them. It'll be fun, you'll see. We'll put it up at your place tomorrow night, okay?"

"Yes, but—"

"Ahh, here's a fine wine," he interrupted, gesturing to the wine list. "One of my favorites."

Chapel listened absently as Ben ordered the wine from the steward, and was vaguely aware of the tasting procedure and Ben's approval of the selection. Her mind was whirling from the events of the past hour. Everything Ben said and did had suddenly taken on gigantic proportions of importance.

The teddy bear was the dearest, sweetest gift she'd ever been given. It spoke volumes, a symbol of what she had never known, never had. And the bear told of yet another side of Ben, a sensitive, whimsical part of him that brought a warm glow to her heart.

And now the Christmas tree. He hadn't really asked if she wanted one, but had simply informed her that was how it would be. Why wasn't she angry at him for being so pushy, for giving her no choice in the matter other than where the tree would be set up? What had happened to her independence, her decision that she alone would determine her own course of action? They had been swept away by Benjamin Simmons and the prospect of a glittering Christmas tree.

Teddy bears, Christmas trees, and Ben, Chapel mused. What was happening to her? She was being caught up in a world she didn't understand, was torn between euphoria and fear. Was she losing her identity, her purpose, the firm belief in who and what she was? What was Ben doing to her?

"Chapel?" Ben said.

"Yes?"

"A toast." He lifted his glass. "To flowers in the spring, to teddy bears, and Christmas trees. To you, Chapel Barclay, and to romance."

Oh, good grief, she was going to cry! Chapel thought, blinking back her tears as she lifted her wineglass. What in heaven's name was the matter with her?

"Are you ready to order, sir?" the waiter asked.

"Chapel?" Ben said.

"What? Oh, yes, of course. I'll have . . . uh, whatever you're having."

Ben's eyes widened, then he placed their orders as Chapel stared out the window. Ben studied her profile and decided something was wrong. He'd bet twenty bucks Chapel had never before turned over her choice of dinner to a man. She was tense, seemed upset. It wasn't the bear. She'd loved the bear. The Christmas tree? Hell, she deserved a tree, the fun, the joy of the holiday season. He wasn't backing off on that one. He'd give her everything that cold-fish mother of hers had denied her. Chapel was his now and— What? Chapel was his now? Did that mean he loved her? Yes! Yes, he loved her!

"I'll be damned," he murmured, a wide grin spreading over his face.

"What?" Chapel asked, redirecting her gaze to him.

"Chapel, what's wrong?" he asked, covering her hand with his on top of the table. "You were so happy before and now, I don't know, you seem edgy."

"No. No, I'm fine."

"I don't think you are. Tell me what's bothering you."

"Oh, Ben," she said, sighing deeply, "it's as though I don't know who I am anymore. Everything changed when I met you, and it's all happened so quickly. Ever since I was a young girl, I've known exactly what I was doing, where I was headed. Now nothing is clear. I'm ecstatically happy one minute and crying the next. Oh, I'm not making a bit of sense."

"Yes, you are," he said, smiling warmly. "It all goes back to the fact that something very special, very beautiful, is happening between us. Now that it's hit me, I'll need time to adjust too."

"Adjust? To what?"

"Love."

"What?"

"I love you, Chapel. I sincerely love you, and I think you have the right to know that."

She stared at him as if she had never seen him before in her entire life. Her heart was beating wildly and a swishing noise filled her ears.

Ben loved her, she thought. He loved her. He loved her.

"No," she whispered, shaking her head.

"Yes," he said firmly, looking directly into her eyes. "I love you. I've waited a long time for you, Chapel, and I've found you. We agreed to discover what was taking place between us, and now I know. It's love. Don't run from it, from me. There's nothing to be frightened of."

"You're assuming a great deal, Ben Simmons," she said sharply, pulling her hand free. "I don't recall saying that I'm in love with you."

"True. Maybe you should get in touch with yourself and find out."

"No! Well, I don't know. What I mean is . . ."

He chuckled. "That was very articulate, counselor. Look, you don't have to say anything one way or the other for now. Just believe that I love you."

"Why?"

"Why what?"

"Why did you fall in love with me? It's very romantic, I suppose, to take a woman to a restaurant like this and declare your love for her. But don't you see? There has to be something more than just a window dressing of romance. There has to be more depth, sharing, communication."

Ben frowned. "You want more from me than the words *I love you*?"

"Those words are sometimes easily spoken, Ben," she said softly.

He let out a deep breath. "I guess really communicating with someone is a lot more complicated than I realized. You're asking me to bare my soul to you."

"I suppose I am."

He stared out the window for a long time as though struggling with his own thoughts. Chapel watched him intently, unaware that she was hardly breathing.

"Okay," he said finally, turning to look at her, "here it is. I guess anyone viewing my life would figure I had it made because of the lucky breaks I've had in the past year. I've worked hard, but I had no control over the public's response to my column. But there was something missing, Chapel. There was an emptiness within me, and I didn't know why or how to fix it. And then I met you. You made me whole again, warmed me, filled me with sunshine instead of darkness. And I fell in love with you. I—Dammit, this isn't communication! This is corny!"

"Is it true?"

"Yeah, it's true, every word. I love you, and I like

you. I think you're beautiful, and I respect your intelligence. Know what? Romance is fun. Communication is exhausting!"

"But it's so important."

"Yeah, well. . . . Look, concentrate on this for now. I, Ben Simmons, am in love with you, Chapel Barclay. That is the truth, and it isn't going to go away. You need to figure out how you feel about that, *and* how you feel about me."

She blinked once slowly, then stood on trembling legs. "Will you excuse me?" she said, her voice weak. "I believe I will go to the powder room."

"Certainly," Ben said solemnly, though amusement flickered through his dark eyes. Good, he thought. She was off to do her thinking thing. She'd get in touch with herself and realize she had nothing to fear. She did care for him. Didn't she? Of course, she did. All the signs were there. But what if she fought an inner battle and decided to ignore that caring, and him? Damn, he could lose his Chapel! "No way," he muttered. "I'm sticking like glue."

He sipped his wine and thought about what he had revealed to her. He had told her things that were deeply personal and private, things he had never shared with another person. And now he felt good, as though a weight had been lifted from his shoulders. Interesting. Very interesting.

Chapel sank onto a velvet chair in the ladies' room and pressed her hands to her burning cheeks. Think! she told herself. Calm down and think. Ben Simmons loved her. Dear Ben, who could very well expect to come home to find her decked out in a big red bow. Oh, ha! Never! He had a lot of nerve, sitting there informing her that she needed to determine her feelings for him. How dare he tell her what to do. Just because she loved him didn't give him—

Chapel gasped. Loved him? Did she love Ben? When had that happened? Why couldn't she have waited until she figured out if she *wanted* to love him first? But, just because she had fallen in love didn't mean she had to do anything about it. Now that she understood why she was acting so flaky, she could regain control of herself and the situation. She'd decide if she wanted to be in love with Ben later.

She marched from the room and slid back onto her chair just as the waiter was preparing to serve their food.

"Doesn't that look delicious?" she said. "And I'm so hungry. Let's eat before it gets cold, Ben." She popped a bite of asparagus into her mouth. "Fantastic."

Ben suppressed his smile and began to eat. So that was how she was going to handle it, he thought. The issue was to be totally ignored. Okay, he'd go along with it, give Chapel time to settle down and adjust. He'd play it her way. For now.

Chapel concentrated on her meal, then stole a look at Ben from beneath her lashes. She nearly choked on her mouthful of prime rib as she watched him eat. The candlelight cast flickering shadows over him, emphasizing his deep tan and the rugged planes of his handsome face, as well as the silky texture of his sun-streaked hair. As he placed the fork in his mouth and his soft, sensuous lips closed over the prongs, Chapel's heart began a two-step.

Candlelight was cheating, she decided. But oh, those lips. She knew those lips. When Ben kissed her, she melted. He was so big and strong, yet so gentle. And his hands. How she adored the feel of them moving over her skin. His entire body was like tempered steel, so hard, while she was soft.

She cleared her throat and shifted in her chair as fingers of desire tingled throughout her. Ben glanced up at her and smiled. Oh, she groaned silently, his smile was too much. It just spread across his face and made his beautiful dark eyes dance a jig. No wonder she'd fallen in love with this man. He was incredible! He was also warm and caring, and had given her an enormous teddy bear. And he'd talked to her, shared his thoughts and feelings. It had been difficult for him to admit to having a void within himself, but he'd done it. He'd gone further than just a romantic interlude for her.

Eat, she told herself. She had firmly decreed that there was nothing romantic about dinner out. But the candlelight really wasn't playing fair!

"You're lovely in the candlelight," Ben said.

"I knew it!" she exclaimed. "Candlelight is straight out of your 'Dear Ben' column. It's a seduction device, a—a tool of your trade."

"Huh?"

"Well, it's true. You recommend cozy dinners for two with candles on the table. Right?"

"Absolutely," he said, nodding. "And I'll tell you why. Everything around us is cloaked in darkness. In our case it's shutting out the other people in this restaurant. There's no one else here but us. For some other couple it might give them a chance to ignore how shabby the furniture is, or to forget the stack of bills sitting on the end table. Right now, Chapel, for me there is no one in this room but you. You're all I can see, you're all I want to see. Candlelight is not a seduction device. It's a romantic message that says you are the most important person to me, and nothing and no one else matters."

"Oh," she said. "I never thought of it like that."

"I know, Chapel, but you'll come to understand love, romantic love, because I'm going to be right here to teach you. I think I have some things to learn about communication too."

Wasn't that the sweetest thing? she thought dreamily. Maybe she'd buy some candles and— No! She wasn't falling for this stuff. Ben was attempting to sweep her off her feet, and Lord knew her body would let him. But what of her mind? Had he asked her about her day, what cases she was working on? There was more to life than sexy candlelight!

"Want to hear about my briefs?" she asked.

His fork stopped in midair. "Chapel, I'd adore hearing about those filmy, lacy little things you wear, but I'd prefer show-and-tell, and this is hardly the place."

"Not those briefs! My legal documents."

"Oh! Oh, sure. Lay it on me. I'm interested in every aspect of your career."

"You are?" she asked, frowning slightly.

"Of course. I love you, every part of you. Tell me about your day."

"Well, actually it was pretty routine, borderline boring. I think your trip to the car factory was more exciting."

"Yeah, it was something. What an operation. They start from nothing and bingo! There's a car. Amazing. They've got this machine that . . ."

Chapel listened intently as Ben described what he had seen on the automobile assembly line. He had a natural flair for making the mundane come alive, and she was soon laughing in delight at his story. The tension ebbed from her body, and she welcomed the strength and warmth of Ben's hand as he covered hers.

And the candlelight continued to glow.

There were no people, no voices, no clatter of dishes. Chapel saw and heard only Ben. She met his tender gaze, and matched him smile for smile. His voice was not a mere voice; it was dark velvet, stroking her with whisper softness. Currents of desire were weaving back and forth between them, pulling them closer together, and further away from reality.

"Chapel," Ben said finally after paying the bill, "let's get out of here."

"Hmm?" she said, smiling at him rather crookedly.

He chuckled, then stood and extended his hand to her. She rose to join him and found no fault in his assisting her with her coat. The icy wind blowing off the river greeted them when they left the restaurant, and Ben pulled her close as they waited for the valet to bring the car around.

"I love you," he murmured, kissing her on the temple.

And she loved him, Chapel thought. But she really didn't want to think about it now.

"Hey, Bear, how's life?" Ben said, when they were in the car.

"He's so cute. Or maybe he's a she."

"You bet it's a she. The only male roommate you'll have is me, madam."

"Oh?"

"If you think that sounds macho, possessive, and slightly chauvinistic, you're right. In my heart, mind, and soul, you are mine."

"You can't own another person, Ben," she said quietly.

"That's not what I'm saying. It's a possessiveness to the point of wanting to be with you through the good times and bad. Understand?"

"I don't know. I guess so."

"Don't worry about it. Everything is going to be fine between us. Everything."

Was it? Chapel wondered. It was easy to say that while they were basking in the aftermath of a romantic evening. But in the harsh reality of a new day? They were so different, she and Ben. She functioned alone, with only a few close friends. Ben was outgoing, enjoyed the spotlight. He wrote a column that she still had qualms about, although he did have a ready answer for the purpose of each piece of advice. She had a career in Detroit. He lived in Santa Fe. So many questions.

Ben parked in the underground garage of Chapel's apartment building, then walked around the car to open her door. The fact that she was already standing outside the car caused him to chuckle.

"Little independent spurt there, huh?" he said, reaching in the back seat for the bear.

Chapel stuck her tongue out at Ben's broad back.

In the elevator they were joined by a man who reeked of alcohol, and who was weaving unsteadily on his feet.

"Hey," the man said, his speech slurred, "I know you two. Saw ya on the tube. Dear Ben and Chapel Somethin'. Watcha doin' together? Didn't think you liked each other much."

"You thought wrong," Ben said, moving between Chapel and the man.

"Oh, I get it," the man said, winking at Ben. "You're doin' your sexy stuff on the frigid lawyer. Gotta red bow handy? Women need to know their place. The bedroom and the kitchen, that's where they belong. Yep. 'Course, you know that, Dear Ben."

"Give it a rest," Ben said tightly.

"Well, hell," the man said, "I'm only saying what you write every day. Must work, 'cause you've defrosted the iceberg here."

Ben shoved the bear at Chapel, then grabbed the man by his lapels and slammed him up against the wall.

"Ben, don't!" Chapel cried. The doors swished open on her floor, and she tugged on Ben's arm. "Come on," she said. "He's not worth it. Ben!"

"Yeah," Ben said, releasing his grip.

"I'll sue!" the man shouted.

"Stuff it!" Ben said, leaving the elevator and stalking down the hall.

In Chapel's living room he shrugged out of his overcoat and practically threw it onto the sofa. He ran his hands through his hair, then began to pace the floor with heavy strides. Chapel removed her coat, then sank onto a chair, watching Ben. The bear sat on the floor and grinned.

"Dammit!" Ben finally said. "How many people interpret my column like that? How many? Hell, even you did, or still do, for all I know. I give every letter—every damn letter I answer—maximum effort, thought, care. For what? To have what I write misconstrued? I get labeled a sexist, an advocate of sexual exploitation!"

"Ben, calm down. The man was drunk. He isn't important."

"That was *you* on *Opposite Views*, Chapel," he said, spinning around to face her. "Hell, you wanted my column banned!"

"Maybe I was wrong."

"Maybe? Just, maybe?"

"I'm trying to understand about romance," she said, her voice rising, "but I can't be expected to grasp it all at once. You said you realized that."

"Why can't you accept me on faith? It suddenly occurs to me that I'm passing tests for you, Chapel. I have to qualify something as simple as a candlelight dinner. What happens if I buy you a filmy nightgown? Do you have me run out of town on a rail?"

"Oh, good grief," she said, folding her arms across her chest and frowning. "This is absurd. You're overreacting to something a drunk said. Surely you've had people find fault with your column in the past, make off-color remarks or whatever."

"Yeah, sure, but . . . do you know what I felt in that elevator? Fear. Fear that you'd listen to that slob, that I'd turn around and see anger in your green eyes again, have you accuse me of trying to exploit you."

"Then where is your trust and belief in *me*?" she asked, jumping to her feet. "I said I was trying to understand you, your world, your column. Am I getting that same understanding in return?"

"Of course, dammit. I love you!"

"Well, dammit," she yelled, "I love you, too, but that doesn't seem to be getting us anywhere! I swear, Ben Simmons, you're getting despicable again."

"What did you say?" he asked in amazement.

"You heard me!"

"I heard you say that you love me," he said, gripping her by the shoulders. "You did say that, Chapel."

"Oh. Well, I . . . Well . . ."

"Do you? Do you love me?"

"Yes!" she said sharply, shrugging out of his grasp. "Yes, all right, I do. What I haven't decided is whether or not I *want* to love you."

"What do you plan to do?" he asked, his jaw tightening. "Push a button and turn it off? That's not how it works. You can't control love like you have every other aspect of your life."

"I certainly can," she said, planting her hands on her hips. "I'm not a dewy-eyed kid, who will allow herself to be carried off on a white charger. *I* determine my destiny. I decide where I'm going, and whether I go there alone. What I've seen so far of love is not overly appealing. It's gotten me a man screaming at me in my living room."

"And a fuzzy bear," he said, grinning at her.

"Oh, no, you don't. Your sexy smile isn't going to melt me down to my socks this time, Benjamin. I admit that I love you, but whether or not I intend to pursue or ignore that emotion has not been decided."

"Jury is still out, huh?" he said, trying to suppress his smile and failing. "You don't mind if I hang around for the verdict, do you?"

"I—"

"Actually I think this is terrific," he went on, pulling off his tie and stuffing it in his pocket. "We'll put our relationship into terms that you can immediately comprehend. I realize now that I haven't been entirely fair to you."

"What?" she said, squinting at him. "What are you talking about?"

"Equal rights, my sweet. I'm pushing the theory of romance at you right and left, because that's what I believe in. But you operate logically, like in a court of law. You need to approach this from a more practical standpoint, weigh and measure both sides of the coin. Love just might not be your cup of tea, and you need to check it out."

"I do?"

"Absolutely. Heavens, you're so intelligent, Chapel. It's amazing, it really is. I never would have thought of this."

"Thought of what?"

"Seeing if we really should be in love." He sighed deeply. "I'm such a romantic. I just followed my heart, my mind be damned. We romantics have a tendency to do that, you know. But you? Well, praise the Lord, we can count on you to be logical and tackle this thing with a clear head. Yes, sir, you are something."

"I don't have the foggiest notion what you're blithering about."

"You don't? Well, that's strange, because it was your idea. You don't know if you want to be in love with me, so we're going to test it out, make sure this is right for us. Romantics go off half cocked at times. It's part of our basic nature. Anyway, I agree to your proposal. I'll move my stuff in here tomorrow."

"What?" she shrieked. "What?"

"Problem?" he asked, eyebrows raised in innocence. "How fair would it be for me to drag you off to romantic restaurants every night? You have the right to view love on your own turf. I plan to cooperate fully because I'm a helluva nice guy. Now, then! You have that look in your eyes that says you need to do your thinking routine. You sit down and think your little heart out and I'll make some coffee."

Chapel sank onto a chair. Her legs refused to hold her for another second. She watched Ben disappear into the kitchen, and all she could think was *Huh?*

After shaking her head as if to clear away the fog, she took a deep breath, let it out slowly, then folded her hands primly in her lap.

What had happened? she wondered. One minute she and Ben were yelling the roof off, and the next the man was planning on moving in with her because she had the right to examine love on her own turf. Did people really say 'turf'? That was beside the point. The fact remained that Ben Simmons was taking up residence in her apartment.

Like hell he was!

Wait a minute, her mind whispered. Was it really all that ridiculous? She *had* fallen prey to that damnable candlelight in the restaurant. If Ben was left in control, he'd channel all his energies toward romance and excerpts from his column. She was more susceptible to that stuff than she'd ever dreamed possible.

And would he continue to communicate, to share with her? She had to know that too. She was an independent career woman, who answered to no man. It could very well be that love had no place in her life, and she would know that if she lived with Ben for a few days. Of course, he should move in with her. It was the only thing to do to equalize their relationship, and remove the total control from his hands. Excellent.

"Okay to come back yet?" Ben called.

"Yes," she said, "it certainly is."

He returned carrying a tray with cups of coffee and a plate of cookies. He set it on the coffee table, presented Chapel with a cup, then sat down on the sofa.

"Hello," he said pleasantly. "Does that smile mean you've come to a conclusion, counselor?"

"I have," she said. "I've decided that you should move in here for a few days. It's the logical, reasonable thing to do, since life is not one continual candlelight dinner."

"Hear, hear," Ben said, raising his cup in salute.

"I concede that we are in love with each other."

"That's very magnanimous of you." He hid his smile by taking a sip of coffee.

"However, that does not automatically guarantee that we *should* be in love with each other."

"I understand perfectly."

"Good."

"Well, I'd better shove off," he said, standing up. "It's getting late, and you have to go to work tomorrow."

"You're leaving?"

"Well, yeah. Let it not be said that Ben Simmons

took advantage of an evening centered on romantic candlelight. Romance is an entity unto itself, and not a foregone conclusion to sex. I would be eligible for the ever-handy label of despicable if I tried to cash in on the candle. Therefore I'm hitting the road."

"Oh," she said, acutely aware of her disappointment as she got to her feet.

"But will I kiss you good night?" he added, pulling her into his arms. "Oh, yes, ma'am. That is definitely on the agenda."

His tongue traced the outline of her lips, then slipped between them as she laced her fingers behind his neck. He nestled her body against his, and his hands roamed in lazy, seductive circles over her back, her buttocks, up her sides to her breasts. The kiss intensified as the fire of need flared between them, heightening their passion.

Ben groaned deep in his chest, and the sound brought an involuntary gasp of pleasure from Chapel. She was awash with desire. Her body was aching for the fulfillment of Ben's vibrant masculinity.

"I want you, Chapel," he murmured, trailing kisses down her throat. "Lord, how I want you. Cancel the candle. Pretend you never saw it. Just think about now, this minute."

"What candle?" she asked dreamily.

"Let me love you, darlin'," he said, nibbling on her ear.

She really should speak to him about that "darlin' " number, she thought. And she would . . . later. "Yes, Ben," she whispered, "love me. Now. I want you, too."

He cradled her face in his hands and kissed her so softly, so lingeringly, that she nearly went limp. In an almost mindless daze she felt herself being lifted and carried into the bedroom. Clothes seemed to float away. Ben's hands and lips, tongue and teeth were everywhere as he lay beside her on the cool sheets.

Their joining was urgent, almost rough. They cried out as ecstasy burst upon them, then clung to each other as they drifted slowly, reluctantly, back to the real world.

"I love you, Chapel," Ben said, kissing her hard and long before moving away. "Curl up here." He drew her against his body.

"So sleepy," she said, wiggling closer to him.

"Then sleep, right here in my arms," he said, kissing her on the forehead. "Good night, my love."

"'Night," she mumbled.

Within minutes Chapel was deeply asleep. Ben slid off the bed and went into the living room to check the lock on the door and turn off the lights. Back in the bedroom, he walked to the window and stared out at the dark, frosty night.

Chapel loved him, he thought. Thank heaven for that much. But it was all so fragile, could splinter into a million pieces at any given moment. She was so wary, and could decide to deny that love and return to the world she knew and understood. He'd bulldozed her about his moving in here, and actually snowed her into believing it had been her idea. Definitely despicable. But hell, he was desperate! He was fighting for his life.

"I can't lose you, darlin'," he said to the night. "I just can't."

Seven

By noon the next day Chapel was mentally babbling. She sat at her desk in her office and went over and over in her mind the amazing turn of events of the past days.

Her life, she decided, was in the blender.

She was in love, and loved in return, which in itself was a jolt to her nervous system. But the capper was that Benjamin Simmons was living in her apartment! Somehow, *somehow*, that plan of action had been her idea, and for the life of her she couldn't figure out how it had happened! But he was there all right. The languorous lovemaking they had shared that morning was definite evidence to that fact. Ben had kissed and caressed her until she was—

"Yes! Well!" she said aloud, shifting in her chair as the heat of desire began to rise within her.

The lovemaking portion of being in love, she mused, was wonderful, fantastic, beyond description. To become one with Ben was a joining not only of bodies, but of souls. To give was to receive. It was man and woman as one, sharing an exquisite journey together. It was . . . absolutely super!

"Okay, okay!" she muttered as a flush crept onto her cheeks. But there was more to this than that.

She rested her elbows on the desk, cupped her chin in her hands, and frowned. The bottom line of her dilemma was whether or not she wanted to be in love. Her well-ordered existence was suddenly off-kilter due to the presence of a man. A man who was capable of drugging her senses and making her lose touch with reality by just walking into the room. Not good. Evenings previously spent working on her legal cases would now be centered on Ben. Emotional energies directed to her law career were being channeled toward Ben. She had the urge to run, yet in the next breath was counting the hours until she could go home to Ben and melt into his arms.

"Love is stinky," she muttered.

"Did you say what I think you said?" Beth asked, entering the office. "Love isn't stinky, it's stupendous. Chapel Barclay, are you in love?"

That did it. Chapel burst into tears.

"Definitely in love," Beth said, gathering a weeping Chapel into her arms and leading her to the sofa.

"Now, then: Who is this phenomenal creature who's managed to bowl you over?"

"You won't believe it," Chapel said, sniffling into a hankie Beth pressed into her hand.

"Try me."

"It's Ben. Ben Simmons. Dear Ben."

"I don't believe it!"

"Oh-h-h," Chapel wailed.

"Sorry. You just took me by surprise," Beth said, patting Chapel's knee. "Does he love you?"

"Yes."

"Oh, how nice! So what's the problem?"

"I don't know if I want to be in love! It's so jarring and unsettling. There's not one iota of logical reasoning involved, and it's confusing. Of course, there are things about it that are wonderful. But then again. . . . Oh, I can't stand this! I wish I'd never met Benjamin Simmons. Never met him? That's awful! I love him! But I don't want to love him! Do I?"

"Goodness," Beth said, "you're a total wreck. I've never seen you like this, Chapel. Of course, you've never been in love before either. You've got to calm down and get a grip on yourself. Blow your nose."

"Do you think I'm losing my mind?"

"No, honey, it was your heart you lost. And I think it was long overdue. You're frightened because it's so new, that's all. Why can't you just take it slow and easy, give yourself time to adjust?"

"Slow and easy? The man is living in my apartment!" Chapel said, then burst into tears again.

"Oh. Whose idea was that?"

"Mine. I think. Yes, it was. I think. Oh, I don't know." She threw up her hands. "Fact remains, Ben is there, and I'm supposed to be viewing love on my own turf so I won't be swayed by the candles."

"What?"

"You know, romance, 'Dear Ben' stuff. Ben feels it's only fair I have a total picture of the whole thing, not just the romantic part that he's so crazy about."

"That's certainly decent of him," Beth said, nodding. "I like Ben."

"And I love him!"

"That's obvious. But you don't know if you want to love him, right?"

"Right," Chapel said, brushing the tears from her cheeks.

"Honey, has it ever occurred to you that you no longer have any choice in the matter?"

"I certainly do have a choice!"

"Chapel, this is not a legal case that you can decide whether or not to take on. Love can't be controlled by a level of intelligence. Cupid doesn't care if you're a genius or a dumb-dumb. You're a goner."

"I refuse to be a goner," Chapel said, jumping to her feet. "My future, my destiny, is mine to determine. If I decide that love is not for me, I'll simply walk away from it and resume my life as it was. Ben will go back to Santa Fe, and I'll never . . . see him again . . . and . . . oh-h-h!"

"I'll get you another hankie," Beth said. "It's going to be a long afternoon."

It was, indeed, a long afternoon, and by the time Chapel stepped off the elevator and walked down the hall to her apartment, she was exhausted. As she began to insert her key in the lock, the door was whisked open, she was hauled inside the room, then kissed very passionately by Ben.

"Hi," he said, smiling down at her, his arms still holding her tightly against him. "You look tired."

"I am," she said, leaning her head against his chest and inhaling his familiar aroma.

"My poor baby. Why don't you change into your fuzzy purple feet? Dinner is in the oven and we'll eat soon."

"You made dinner?" she asked, lifting her head to look at him. "I— Oh, Lord! What is that?"

"Our Christmas tree," he said, obviously proud of himself. "It's a beauty, isn't it?"

Chapel's mouth dropped open as she moved out of Ben's arms and walked slowly forward. The tree was enormous. It nearly touched the ceiling and was so wide that Ben had had to push the sofa and chairs out of the way. The fragrance of pine permeated the air.

"What happened to the tiny tabletop type?" she asked, staring at the tree.

"I couldn't relate to those."

"But—"

"I got tons of decorations. As soon as we eat and you relax a bit, we'll get started. You like it, don't you? I had to carry it up the back stairs because it wouldn't fit in the elevator. I nearly killed myself, but it was worth it. You do like it, don't you?"

She turned to him with every intention of telling him to haul that monstrosity out of her living room, but the words never came. Ben had his hands shoved into the pockets of his jeans, and he was frowning slightly. He seemed to be searching her face for approval, for assurance that she did like the tree he had worked so hard to provide for her. Her heart did a funny little tap dance, and she smiled.

"It's a beautiful tree, Ben," she said. "Thank you. I'll go change, we'll eat, then we'll decorate it. It will be the prettiest tree in Detroit." She walked over to him and gently kissed him. "Thank you very, very much."

Ben watched as she went into the bedroom, then let out a rush of air in relief. It had been touch-and-go there for a minute, but she loved the tree. She deserved the best Christmas tree in town. She really looked beat this evening too. At least he had a nourishing dinner waiting for her, but he didn't like her working so hard. If they were married. . . . Married? Yes, married! She could lighten her load then, but would she? Her career had been all she had known. Would she be willing to strike a new balance, allow time for him, for them? And where would they live? Detroit was so damn big and cold. He liked Santa Fe, but would Chapel? And how did she feel about babies? They certainly had a lot to figure out, and that would call for a great deal of communication. But they loved each other, and for now that was enough.

In the bedroom, Chapel opened her closet door to reach for a pair of jeans, then stopped as she saw Ben's clothes hanging next to hers. Tentatively she ran her hand down the sleeve of a dark gray shirt. The few shirts and trousers had price tags dangling from them, and she surmised that Ben had gone shopping to increase his wardrobe from what he had orginally brought for his brief stay in Detroit.

Never in her entire life had a man's belongings nestled close to hers in a closet. It was intimate, she decided, because they were proof that Ben lived here with her. It certainly was official now, that was for sure. And how did she feel about it?

"I'm asking *me*?" she muttered as she grabbed her jeans. Well, it *had* been nice to come home to someone. To be greeted with a kiss, told she looked tired and should relax, and that dinner was already made. It would take a crazy person to find fault with any of that! But it wasn't a true picture of marriage or living together. The woman was expected to perform all the tasks that Ben had done. He was on vacation and messing around in the role of house-husband. The premise of his living here made sense, but the scenario itself was far from realistic.

In the bathroom Chapel again hesitated when she saw Ben's shaving equipment and toothbrush on the shelf. His toothbrush was blue, hers was pink, and there they were, side by side. In what she determined was an act of independence, Chapel separated the two with a tube of toothpaste.

After changing her clothes, brushing her hair free, and pushing her feet into the gigantic purple slippers, she returned to the living room. Her gaze immediately fell on the fragrant tree and she shook her head.

Nobody in their right mind, she decided, bought a tree that big for an apartment the size of hers. But Ben had. No tabletop type for him. It was absurd, totally impractical, and so sweet, it was enough to bring tears to her eyes. What was she going to do with him?

"Chapel?" he called from the kitchen. "Dinner is on the table."

Her eyes widened when she entered the kitchen. Ben had prepared chicken, rice, gravy, and string beans. The table was set, and the paper flowers had a place of honor in the center.

"What should I do to help?" she asked.

"Nothing," he said, filling their coffee cups. "Just sit and enjoy."

She slid onto her chair and waited until Ben sat opposite her. He smiled at her, then nodded toward the steaming food.

"Dig in," he said.

"How did you learn to cook like this?" she asked, filling her plate.

"When I was about fourteen, my mom broke her leg. Dad and I took over the running of the house. We had some real disastrous meals at first, but we got the hang of it."

"But it was only temporary."

"Well, yeah. My mom shooed us out of her kitchen once she was back on her feet. Did you notice there're no lumps in my gravy?"

"Yes, and everything is delicious, Ben."

"Thank you, ma'am."

"When you and your father were in charge of things, did you feel you were doing woman's work? You know, performing tasks that weren't really yours to do?"

"I don't remember," he said, lifting his shoulder in a shrug. "It was a long time ago. Why?"

"Because this isn't realistic, Ben. The purpose of your moving in here was to give me a clear picture of love on an ongoing basis. You're on vacation with no pressures, no deadlines. So you cooked dinner for a lack of something better to do. If you had worked all day, I feel that you would have expected to have a hot meal prepared for you."

"No, I wouldn't. Not if the other person worked outside the house too. We'd fix it together, or eat out, or take turns. I like to cook. I'm not crazy about doing the laundry though. I'll make you a deal. I'll fix your dinner, you wash my socks. Good plan, huh?"

"You have an answer for everything."

"Because there *is* an answer for everything. It's simply a matter of figuring out the best course of action. I realize I'm on vacation and— Okay. I'll rent a typewriter, have my editor Express-Mail me some of Dear Ben's stuff, and earn my keep. Is that closer to normal?"

"I guess it's not fair of me to ask you to work while you're on vacation."

"Darlin', I'll do anything to get you to realize that being in love with me is a nice place to be. Don't you see, Chapel? There's nothing too big for us to work out. We love each other, and we'll compromise, give and take, get it perfect."

"And communicate?"

"I'm working on that. I think there's a fine line between sharing and the right to keep some thoughts private."

"Not if those thoughts affect your actions or attitudes toward the other person, Ben."

"Good point," he said, nodding.

"In all those columns where you suggested romantic settings for couples, you never once implied that they should talk, discuss their problems, in addition to . . . whatever."

"They probably wouldn't have time," he said, grinning and wiggling his eyebrows.

"Darn it, Ben! You're not listening to a word I'm saying."

"Yes, I am listening! Look, I realize you're having difficulty adjusting to all of this, but you seem to be going out of your way looking for trouble."

"I am not! I'm simply attempting to keep a clear picture in my mind of what being in love entails. At what point do we get to the big red bows?" she asked, her voice rising.

He slouched back in his chair, crossed his arms over his chest, and stared at her. "You're still bugged about the red bows, aren't you?" he said. "I've explained the romantic message that bow conveys, but you won't give an inch. If I'd had a candle burning on this table, would you have gotten in a flak about that? Why are you fighting me so hard? Is it independence . . . or is it fear? Fear of the unknown, something you can't control. I said I'd give you time, and I will, but I have to know what I'm battling."

Quick tears blurred Chapel's vision, and she averted her eyes from Ben's. Picking up a spoon she absently traced a pattern on the tabletop as clamoring voices echoed in her mind. Yes, she was afraid of being in love! she admitted silently. Afraid of passing the very essence of her being into Ben's care, of shifting her priorities, her goals, to center on him. Afraid of leaving herself vulnerable, and open to pain if their relationship didn't go as planned. Alone would become loneliness. And she would cry.

But to reveal her fears to Ben would be to strip herself bare. She had told him that she simply didn't know if she wanted to be in love, if it would fit into her well-ordered, logical life. He mustn't know she was afraid.

"Chapel?"

"I told you," she said, still not looking at him. "My life is on the course I chose years ago. I'm simply not positive that love fits into my scheme of things. I will not be dictated to by my emotions, Ben. If I decide not to be in love, then that will be that."

"I see," Ben said, nodding his head. Nice speech, but a bunch of bull, he thought. Chapel was scared to death of loving him. She knew it, but she was not apparently going to tell him the truth. She was copping out on her own stand on communication. Well, he couldn't shake it out of her, so he'd have to be patient and wait. Fear was a large stumbling block, but he'd win. He had to!

Chapel slowly lifted her lashes to find Ben calmly polishing off the remainder of his dinner. He appeared relaxed, as though the topic of conversation had been the weather. So be it. Ben was accepting her explanation, and she was grateful for that. If he had pushed her on the subject of her fear of loving him, she would have burst into tears.

"I'll put the lights on the tree," he said. "It's a one man job. Then we'll decorate it together."

"All right. I'll clean up the kitchen."

"Fair enough," he said, as they both got to their feet. "But first . . . dessert."

"Which is?"

"You." He gathered her close to his chest and covered her mouth with his.

Ben Simmons tasted better than chocolate eclairs, Chapel thought, returning the kiss with total abandonment. He was absolutely delicious.

"Whew!" he said when he lifted his head. "You're potent stuff, lady. Quit kissing me. I've got a tree to trim."

"Yes, sir," she said, smiling up at him. "I'll be along in a few minutes."

"Good." He kissed the end of her nose, then left the kitchen.

Chapel placed her hand on her heart to check if it had returned to at least a reasonable rate, then started to put away the remaining food. She firmly pushed her distressing, confusing thoughts to a dark corner of her mind and concentrated on the Christmas tree.

It had been so many years since she'd been caught up in the festivities of the holiday. She didn't totally ignore it, but merely skimmed around the edges, giving gifts, sending out a few cards. Yet this year there was a huge tree in her living room being guarded by a pink and white bear. And there was Ben.

With a sudden burst of energy she hurried through the chores, and in record time joined Ben in the living room.

"I'm here," she said with excitement. "What's first?"

"You can unpack the ornaments. I'm almost finished with the lights."

"Aren't you going to turn them on?"

"Nope. I checked each string, but we'll wait until we're finished to plug it in."

"Just like Rockefeller Center."

"Yep. You know, I love Christmas trees. They're right up there on the list with flowers in the spring."

Chapel began to unpack the ornaments eagerly. Ben flicked on the radio and Christmas carols filled the air. When he burst into song, Chapel joined him, singing just as poorly and matching him smile for smile. Ornament after ornament was placed on the tree, transforming the bare branches into glittering beauty. Ben lifted Chapel by the waist so she could place the angel on the top, and she tingled with desire as he slid her slowly down his body until her feet touched the floor. They laughed and talked and sang. They had a marvelous time.

"Ready?" Ben finally asked. "I'm going to plug in the lights."

"Yes!" she said, and a moment later gasped in delight. "Oh, Ben," she whispered, "it's so beautiful."

Ben turned off the lamps, then pulled her back against him, wrapping his arms around her as they stood in the glow of the magnificent tree.

"Our first Christmas tree," he said in a low voice. "Tonight will hold very special memories for me, Chapel."

"For me too," she said, turning in his arms to face him. "Thank you for the tree. I'd forgotten how much joy there is in the holidays."

"*You* are my joy," he said, lowering his head to hers.

On the plush carpet, with the rainbow colors of the tree lights dancing over the glistening skin of their naked bodies, they made love. Slowly, sensuously, they touched and kissed each other, igniting passions to raging flames. They prolonged the sweet torment, anticipating the moment of ecstasy, of joining, until they could bear no more. Then they soared high above the earth, clinging to each other as they spilled over the edge into oblivion and lingered there, suspended in time, and space, and love.

Finally, reluctantly, Ben moved away, then reached for the afghan on the back of the sofa and draped it over them. Chapel lay in the crook of his arm, her gaze lingering on the tree.

"I'm going to leave it up forever," she said.

"Oh, yeah?" He chuckled. "You'll change your tune when you're sloshing through pine needles."

"I feel like I did the night of the blizzard, as though we're the only two people in the universe."

"We are." He kissed her on the temple. "Oh, and our bear, of course. The three of us make a dashing family."

"Unusual anyway. But then, you and I aren't a very ordinary couple to begin with."

"What do you mean?" he asked, sifting his fingers through her silky hair.

"We're very different, Ben. You're outgoing, sociable, have no qualms about being recognized in public. I'm a private person, and I don't allow too many people to get close to me. And well, you exist just on the edge of a fantasy world."

"A what?"

"You honestly believe that romance is going to make a tremendous difference in people's lives. This moment, here, in the glow of our tree is romantic. I admit that."

"Score one for the kid from Santa Fe," he said, nibbling on her ear.

"The point is, that in a little while we'll have to move or we'll freeze to death. Then, tomorrow morning it's back to business as usual."

"Wrong. No one can take the memory of tonight from us. It was romantic, heavenly, and ours. We can pull it out and relive it next July, if we want to. You have so much data stored in that brain of yours. Don't you have room for lovely memories?"

"Well, I guess so."

"Good."

"But what about tomorrow?"

"Wait until it becomes today, stir in some romance, a lot of lovin', and we've got it made."

"But—"

"Enough. I'm kissing you."

"You are?"

"Pay attention, Dr. Barclay. I'd hate to have you miss this."

Not the smallest detail of Ben's lovemaking escaped Chapel, and she savored each glorious moment they shared. Another memory, she thought dreamily, when he finally carried her into the bedroom.

Ben laid her on the bed, stretched out next to her, and tucked the blankets carefully around her. When he was sure she was asleep, he left the room and closed the door behind him. After pulling on his jeans, he lifted the receiver to the telephone, dialed the operator, and gave her his credit card number and the number he wanted to call. He drummed his fingers impatiently on the end table as he waited for the connection to be made, then as the phone on the other end started ringing.

"Hello?" a woman's voice finally said.

"Austin?" he said, sitting straight up. "It's Ben."

"Benny? It has to be the middle of the night over there. What's wrong?"

"Austin, I—I'm in love."

"Really? Oh, Benny, that's wonderful. Is she someone I know?"

"No, I'm not in Santa Fe, I'm in Detroit. Austin, I really need your help. Chapel—her name is Chapel Barclay—is a brilliant lawyer and economist. She's a feminist, a very organized, logical woman."

"Does she love you?"

"Yes. Thing is, Austin, she's not sure she wants to be in love. Even more, the whole thing scares the socks off her, but she won't admit it. She's not open, outgoing like you are. She's a very private person. I love her so much, Austin, but I sure as hell could lose her if I can't convince her not to run from me, from what we have. What am I going to do? And don't tell me to write to Dear Ben for advice."

"Dear Ben would say romance is the key, sweet Benny. Why aren't you pulling out all the stops?"

"I have to go easy with the romance, Austin. Chapel thinks it's borderline cheating."

"Oh, pooh, I don't believe it. Chapel may find romantic overtures a bit disconcerting if she's never been the recipient of them before, but she's still a woman. I know you, Benny. You believe in romance, so everything you do would be honest. Go with your instincts. Follow Dear Ben's advice to the letter."

"Think so?"

"Know so. If you love Chapel, that means she's special. Give her a chance to discover who she is as a woman in love. We change when love comes, and it certainly can be frightening. I almost lost Patrick because of my fears. Be yourself, Benny, just as you are. And be patient."

"Yeah. Yeah, okay."

"I love you, darling friend. Keep me posted. Good luck."

"Thanks, Austin. You're my sweetheart. Bye."

Ben replaced the receiver, then laced his fingers behind his head and stared up at the ceiling. Go with his instincts, huh? Pull out all the stops. Be himself, which meant romance by the bucketful. It was very risky, but he wasn't doing so hot by treading softly around Chapel. Every time he got her to relax, her mind snapped into action and she started questioning things. She worried about the tomorrows instead of concentrating on today. He was walking on thin ice, and he knew it. At any given moment she could tell him to take a hike back to Santa Fe. If her fears won, he'd lose. He wasn't going to let that happen!

He had been stifling some of his own romantic inclinations so as not to upset Chapel. That was bad. Their relationship should be based on honesty, everything up front. He would be himself, and give her plenty of time and space to work through her own reactions as they hit her. This was getting complicated, but it was definitely worth it.

Ben patted the smiling bear on the head, unplugged the tree lights, and made his way cautiously through the darkness toward the bedroom. The expletives he cut loose with when he stubbed his toe would have shocked the loyal following of Dear Ben.

Eight

Chapel prided herself on the fact that she had an extremely productive morning at the office. Beth had obviously wanted an update on Ben Simmons, but Chapel had immediately requested several files, ignoring Beth's sigh of frustration. Chapel worked diligently and only thought of Ben approximately every fifteen minutes, which proved, she decided, that she was regaining control of her mind.

Ben had groaned when the alarm had gone off, then buried his head under the pillow. Chapel had left the coffee set on warm so it would be ready when he surfaced, then left him a note wishing him a nice day. The fact that she had anchored the note on the table with the paper flowers held no particular significance, she'd told herself. Nor was it important that she had nearly been late because she had stood gazing at the Christmas tree, replaying in her mind the glorious events of the previous evening.

She was dressed in a tweed suit, and her hair was in a tight chignon. She was Dr. Chapel Barclay, attorney-at-law, in charge, in control, and—well, yes—in love. But that love, should she decide to pursue it, would have to know its place. It would not be allowed to consume her, reduce her to tears, or turn her into a blithering idiot. Her absurd behavior regarding Ben and their relationship was at an end. She would approach this emotional catastrophe logically, reasonably, and with class.

"So there," she said. She had to quit saying that. It was so-o-o immature!

Ben stepped out of the elevator and walked down the hall, checking the names on the doors.

"There's my darlin'," he finally said, pushing open a door and entering a nicely decorated reception area.

"Hello," Beth said. "May I help you?"

"Hi," Ben said. "I'd like to see Chapel."

"Do you have an appointment, Mr. . . . ? Oh, wait a minute. I recognize you. You're Ben Simmons—Dear Ben."

"Yep," he said, smiling at her. "You must be the lady of the answering machine. It's nice to meet you."

"Beth Kolb," she said, "and the pleasure is mine. Is Chapel expecting you?"

"No, this is a surprise. I have here"—he patted the wicker basket under his arm—"a picnic lunch."

"Oh, how divine," Beth said, sighing. "And romantic."

"I try," he said, smiling smugly.

"Beth," Chapel said, coming out of her office, "would you please pull the file on—Ben! What—what are you doing here?"

"Hi, darlin'. I came to take you on a picnic."

"What?"

"Relatively speaking. It's too cold outside, so we'll wing it in your office. Neat, huh?"

"That's crazy! We can't have a picnic here."

"Why not?" Beth asked.

"Yeah, why not?" Ben said. "It'll be fun, cozy, and romantic."

"No, absolutely not," Chapel said, shaking her head. "This is a law office, not a park."

"You have to use your imagination," Ben said. "I'll make bird noises to get you in the mood."

"Carry on," Beth said, flicking on the answering machine. "I have errands to run. The place is yours for the next hour."

"You're a sweetheart," Ben said, kissing Beth on the cheek. She blushed a pretty pink. "Come along, darlin'," he said, taking Chapel's arm. "Time's a-wastin'."

"But . . . but . . ." Chapel sputtered, as Ben hauled her into her office and pushed the door closed with his foot.

Beth laughed in delight.

Ben set the wicker basket on the sofa, removed a tablecloth, and whipped it over the coffee table with a flourish. When he tossed his overcoat on a chair and began to place containers of food on the table, Chapel found her voice.

"Ben, stop that!" she said. "We are not having a picnic here!"

"Sure we are. We have to eat lunch, so why not do it with a little sparkle, a little—"

"Romance," she said, rolling her eyes to the heavens.

"Absolutely." He settled onto the floor. "Sit," he said, patting the carpet next to him. "I've got some great goodies here."

Chapel planted her hands on her hips, squinted at Ben, and tapped her foot.

"Are you doing your thinking thing?" he asked.

"Yes! So please be quiet."

"Got it," he said, and popped an olive into his mouth.

Benjamin Simmons was a looney tune, Chapel thought. He was totally bonkers! And rude. How dare he turn her office into a zoo. Well, a park, not a zoo, but still, he was being despicable again! A picnic, for crying out loud! How long had it been since she'd been on a picnic? Years, many, many years.

Ben had certainly brought some delicious-looking food, and she did have to eat. She was probably the only woman in Detroit having a picnic that day with her lover. It did show an awful lot of imagination on Ben's part. And caring. And that tender, whimsical part of him that believed in fuzzy bears, Christmas trees, and . . . romance. She'd never had a birthday party, let alone a picnic created just for her. It might be fun.

She laughed, slipped off her shoes, and dropped to her knees beside Ben.

"Don't you dare eat all those olives, Ben Simmons," she said, teasing.

"Hello, my Chapel," he said, and pulled her close, claiming her mouth with his.

She wrapped her arms around his neck and returned the kiss, melting against him, savoring his warmth and strength. Oh, he felt so good, smelled so good, and tasted so good, like tangy olives. He was Ben, he was here, and they were having a picnic!

"Chapel," he murmured, trailing kisses down her slender neck.

He pulled the pins from her hair, and gently spread the cinnamon-colored cascade over her shoulders. Her jacket was slipped away, then Ben kissed her again, his hands roaming over her silky blouse. Her breasts became heavy, aching for more of his tantalizing touch, as a pulsing heat began in the core of her femininity.

The room disappeared into a hazy mist. Birds were singing, a breeze was dancing through leaves on trees, butterflies flitted from flower to flower. Their fragrance permeated the air, drugging Chapel's senses as Ben's lips, tongue, and hands wreaked havoc with her touch with reality.

"Ben," she gasped.

"What?" His voice was hoarse with passion. "Oh. Right."

He moved her carefully away from him and drew a shuddering breath as he strove for control. He smiled weakly, then ran his hand down his face.

"Whew!" he said. "You are really something. I kiss

you, touch you, and I'm gone. Eat an olive while I tell
my body to go on temporary hold. Ah, Chapel." He
placed his hand on her cheek. "I love you so much."

A lump formed in Chapel's throat, and she blinked
back her tears as she turned her head to rest her lips
against the warm palm of his hand. Their eyes met,
and messages of love were sent and received. Time
lost meaning as neither moved, not wishing to break
the wondrous spell of awareness, desire, infinite joy.
It was a moment that created a memory, and they
smiled.

"Lunch," Ben said finally, slowly taking his hand
from her cheek.

"Thank you for my picnic," she said, her voice
trembling. "It's a wonderful surprise."

"My pleasure, my lady. Let's sample this stuff. I got
it at a deli, and I can't guarantee what it all is."

"I'll try some of everything. It will be an adventure,"
she said, beginning to fill her plate.

Ben kept silent, but his heart was thundering in
his chest, overflowing with love for this complicated,
vulnerable, beautiful woman.

Inch by emotional inch she was growing, blos-
soming into a delicate flower, each petal further evidence of whom she was becoming, the discoveries
she was making about who she really was. She had so
much, so very much, within her. Lord, how he loved
her!

"Ben? Why aren't you eating?" she asked.

"What? Oh, I'm waiting to see if you'll leave me
any."

"I can't resist. It all looks so scrumptious," she

said, laughing merrily. "And just think. We don't have to worry about ants."

He smiled and filled his plate. As they ate he asked her about the cases she was working on, complimented the decor of the office, and told her that her grandmother, who doubled as a secretary, was a neat lady.

Chapel basked in his attention. She knew without a flicker of a doubt that he was sincerely listening to what she said. She was glowing with happiness, and her heart nearly burst with love for Benjamin Simmons.

"I guess I should be going," he finally said. "Let you get back to work."

"I'll help you pack up the food. Oh, Ben, it was all so lovely. Thank you."

"You're welcome," he said, kissing her quickly. "I enjoyed it very much."

They repacked the basket, then Ben shrugged into his coat. He pulled Chapel into his arms and kissed her until she was trembling.

"See you at home," he said, his mouth still against hers.

"Yes," she said, then watched as he walked from the room.

After he had left she stood motionless, filling her senses with his lingering aroma. Then she snapped herself out of her trance, picked up her hairpins off the carpet, and went into the bathroom. Staring at her reflection in the mirror, she gasped softly at what she saw. Her cheeks were flushed, her lips slightly swollen from Ben's passionate kisses, her eyes bright and sparkling. Her hair was in wild disarray. She looked and felt alive, and in love.

And it was glorious.

She brushed her hair, then started to twist it into the usual chignon, only to hesitate. Why not leave it loose? She had appointments that afternoon, but her hairstyle had nothing to do with her efficiency as a lawyer. Yes, she'd allow herself a reprieve from that tight bun on her neck. Maybe she'd leave her jacket off too. Her blouse was pretty, so why not let it be seen?

She walked into the front office and flicked off the answering machine. Beth entered a moment later and stopped in her tracks. Her gaze swept over Chapel, and a knowing smile tugged onto her lips.

"Enjoy your picnic?" Beth asked.

"Yes, it was wonderful," Chapel said.

"Romantic?"

"Well, I . . . Yes, okay, romantic," Chapel said, laughing. "I can't deny that. Ben made me feel very special, very loved. The overall picture of our relationship is still confusing, but I refuse to dwell on it today."

"Hooray for you. Honestly, Chapel, Ben is incredible. A picnic in December. Goodness. And he's so handsome. My dear girl, you have yourself one fantastic man there. There is so much happiness within your grasp. Reach out for it, honey, and hold on tight."

"We'll see," she said quietly.

"I'm here if you need me. I hope you know that."

"I do, and I thank you. Beth, my mother raised me with the philosophy of doing everything alone. I'm beginning to think that maybe she was wrong. I'm not sure, but just maybe she was wrong."

Back in Chapel's apartment Ben stretched out on the sofa and stared at the ceiling. He was aging fast, he thought. Despite his seemingly calm, casual entrance into Chapel's office, he had been a nervous wreck! And just like the Christmas tree, it had been touch-and-go at the onset. But once Chapel had accepted the idea of the picnic, she had been fantastic. He'd wanted to make love to her right there on the carpet in her office. Once again she had been a combination of little girl and soft, sensuous woman. He'd chalked up one more score on the romantic side of the board. So far, so good. But he still had a long road to travel.

He swung his feet to the floor, reached for the telephone, and called Joe McBride in New York. The agent was disappointed that Ben wouldn't be joining him for the holidays, then asked when Ben would be free to travel. There were offers of more talk-show interviews, as well as a long list of groups wishing Ben to speak.

"I don't know, Joe," Ben said. "Can't it all keep until after the first of the year?"

"I suppose, but some of these are sweet deals that you could lose out on. How much of a vacation do you need?"

"It's not that. I'm involved in something that has to have my undivided attention."

"A woman. Has to be a Santa Fe filly."

"I'm not in Santa Fe. I'm still in Detroit."

"No kidding? Whoever she is, she must have really knocked you over fast."

"You'd better believe it, Joe my boy."

"I'd like to be a mouse in the corner and watch you in action, Dear Ben. Would probably be awesome. Okay, concentrate on your lady, and I'll book you for right after New Year's."

"Well, all right."

"Give me a phone number where I can reach you so I can clear all this with you."

Ben rattled off Chapel's name and number, wished Joe a merry Christmas, then hung up the phone. He drummed his fingers on the end table and frowned. Suddenly he had a time limit on convincing Chapel to marry him. He did not want to flit across the country for various engagements with things unsettled between them. To leave her alone with her fears and confusion would be a terrible mistake.

So, he'd have to make every second count. He'd told her he'd have some "Dear Ben" mail expressed to him to provide a more realistic picture of two people with careers. He'd call Cappy at the *Santa Fe Sun* right away and ask him to bundle up a batch of letters. Fine.

But, he wondered as he stood up, would Chapel consider moving to Santa Fe? He'd be asking her to chuck her law practice and start over. But, dammit, he hated Detroit. The weather was the pits, and he got claustrophobia from all the towering buildings. It was too big, noisy, and fast paced for him. The West was his home, where he belonged. He wanted to raise his children there in the beauty of the desert, sur-rounded by people whose temperaments he understood and respected. Hell, the cavemen were lucky. They just threw their women over their shoulders and toted them off! Caveman tactics with Chapel Barclay would land him in a body cast!

"Bear," he said to the smiling toy, "I sure wish you had a brain in that fuzzy head of yours. I need all the help I can get! Wait a minute! I've got an idea!"

Chapel stepped out of the elevator on her floor in the apartment building and walked slowly down the hall. Last night she'd come home to a gigantic Christmas tree. This afternoon it had been a picnic. Surely Ben didn't have something on the agenda for this evening, did he? No, even Dear Ben would be content with one spurt of romance a day. Wouldn't he? Problem was, she didn't really know which she wanted. A quiet evening at home, or another one of Ben's surprises? No sense in thinking about it. She was never asked for an opinion before something happened!

She unlocked the door and pushed it open, waited a moment to see if she was going to be whisked off her feet, then entered the apartment.

"Chapel? That you?" Ben called from the kitchen.

"Yes. Oh, dear, now what?" she asked, walking forward.

"Hi, darlin'," he said, coming up behind her and nuzzling her neck. "Did you leave your hair loose all afternoon? Fantastic."

"Why is there a movie projector and screen sitting here?"

"'Cause we're going to watch a flick. I would have

gotten a VCR, but this kind of film only comes on the old-fashioned reels."

"Ben Simmons," she said, turning to face him, "is that a dirty movie? I refuse to take part in some kinky—"

"No! No, it's nothing like that. Go change into your purple feet so we can eat."

"Mmm," she said, giving him a suspicious look before heading for the bedroom.

Dinner was hamburgers, french fries, and silence. Chapel watched Ben from beneath her lashes and decided he was definitely nervous. He wolfed down his dinner as though he were a starving man, then concentrated on stirring his coffee. That in itself was ridiculous, as he drank his coffee black. When her last french fry was halfway to her mouth, he whisked her plate off the table and jammed it in the dishwasher.

"Ben, for heaven's sake," she said, "what is—"

"Done," he said, running the sponge over the table. "Movie time. Come on."

"I wouldn't miss this for the world," she muttered.

Ben stopped only long enough to plug in the tree lights, then deposited Chapel in a chair facing the screen.

"Good evening," he said clearing his throat. "We are gathered here tonight to—"

"We who?" she asked.

"You, me, and Bear. Chapel, this is serious business."

"Sorry. Carry on."

"Where was I?"

"We were gathered."

"Oh, yes. It is my pleasure and privilege to take you on a personally conducted tour of Santa Fe, New Mexico."

"Why?"

"Why?" he repeated, frowning. "Because you've never seen it, have you?"

"Well, no, but—"

"You'll be crazy about it. It's where the love of your life was born and raised, remember?"

"Who?"

"Me!"

"Yes, I realize you're from Santa Fe, but—"

"Santa Fe," Ben boomed, causing Chapel to jump, "is the state capital of New Mexico, and is the second oldest city in the United States."

"What's the first oldest city?"

"How in the hell should I know?" he said, none too quietly.

"Good grief, why are you yelling?"

"Let's just watch the movie, okay?" he said, stalking behind the projector.

"Okay," Chapel said pleasantly, folding her hands in her lap.

Ben flicked a switch and a whirring noise filled the air. A series of upside-down letters danced up the screen, then a blurry black-and-white picture appeared.

"Santa Fe, New Mexico," a wobbly voice said.

"It even has sound," Chapel said. "How classy."

"I think he's gargling," Ben said.

"Great changes have taken place here," the voice said, "and now in this year of 1935, Santa Fe is—"

"What?" Ben yelled. "What year?"

"1935," Chapel said.

"Dammit to hell!" He turned off the projector.

"Aren't we going to watch it?"

"No! Chapel, I was trying to show you where I live, how beautiful it is, how much there is to do and see. I'd rather take you there myself, but I thought this would at least give you an idea of what it's like. Nineteen thirty-five. Damn."

She got slowly to her feet, her eyes wide as she looked at Ben.

"Why is it so important to you that I'm impressed with Santa Fe? Ben, are you saying you want me to—"

"Move there. Marry me and come home with me to Santa Fe," he said, his voice low.

"Marry you?" she whispered.

"Yes. I love you, Chapel. I want you to be my wife, the mother of my children. Santa Fe is my home, and it will be yours too."

"Leave Detroit? My law practice? Everything I've worked so hard for?"

"There are lawyers in New Mexico. You could open an office and—"

"Start over from scratch?" she said, her voice rising. "Do you know how long it takes to build a reputation as an honest, competent attorney? Why couldn't you stay here? Dear Ben's mail could be forwarded to you."

"Because I don't like it here! It's too big, the weather stinks, it's crowded, the buildings are going to fall down. You'd love Santa Fe, Chapel. It has flowers in the spring and—"

"I don't believe this! You really expect me to follow

you across the country? Give up all that I have? Just pack up and go like a dutiful little wife?"

"No, as a loving wife, who's willing to relocate with her husband, start a new life with him."

"Why me? Why can't you be the one to move?"

"Because I'm the man!" he said. And that, he thought an instant later, was the dumbest thing he'd ever said. He was definitely, *definitely*, a dead person!

He almost cringed as he watched Chapel's fury build. She planted her hands on her hips, narrowed her eyes, and pursed her lips together. Her face began to turn the same shade as her hair, and he wondered frantically if she was holding her breath. If she became the color of her purple feet, he was going to smack her back to life! Never in his entire years had Benjamin Simmons seen such an angry woman!

"You . . ." she said, expelling a rush of air, "are . . . despicable!"

"Now, darlin', calm down. I didn't mean that quite the way—"

"And don't call me darlin'!" She spun around and marched out of the apartment, slamming the door behind her.

Ben opened his mouth, shut it again, and shook his head in amazement. She'd screwed it up! Chapel had been in such a snit, she'd done everything backward. She was supposed to throw *him* out of there, not vice versa!

"Oh, man," he said, whooping with laughter, "what a funny bit. Okay, dar-r-r-lin', how are you going to get back in here with your dignity intact?"

He sat down on the sofa, crossed his arms over his chest, and waited.

In the corridor Chapel stood ramrod stiff, her hands clutched at her sides in tight fists as she forced herself to mentally count to ten.

Now she was calm, she told herself when she reached ten. Yes, calm. She was also standing out in the hall! Oh, for Pete's sake, she couldn't even flounce from a room in a temper tantrum without going through the wrong door! How embarrassing. She should have ended up in her bedroom, not the hall. Well, there was no way she was turning around and going back in and giving Ben the satisfaction of showing she'd blown it.

She stomped down the hall in her purple slippers, then poked the button for the elevator with more force than was necessary. When the doors swished open she entered, nodding absently at two elderly women, who were bundled up in heavy coats.

"Good evening," one of the women said pleasantly, then shifted her gaze to Chapel's feet. "Those are . . . interesting shoes."

"These?" Chapel said, peering down. "Yes, aren't they? I save them for special occasions like this when I'm going visiting."

"How nice," the woman said, and nearly dragged her companion off the elevator when it stopped at another floor.

Chapel pushed a button and the elevator jolted upward. She tapped her furry foot in angry frustration and concentrated on Ben. Words like *chauvinistic*, *overbearing*, and *presumptuous* came to her mind, and she scowled. But her fury began to cool, and she felt more hurt and disappointment at Ben's easy dismissal of her hard-earned, well-respected career.

Then again, she mused, jabbing another button as she reached her destination, Ben had gone to considerable effort to convince her that Santa Fe was a terrific place to live. The look on his face when he had discovered that his famous flick was as old as the hills had been priceless. It had been a rather nice gesture on his part to do a show-and-tell routine about the area of the country he so dearly loved. It was as though he were trying to ease her into the idea slowly, gently, instead of shoving it down her throat. And he *had* seemed immediately contrite over his sexist statement.

"Mmmm," she said thoughtfully, pushing three buttons at once. Truth of the matter was, she'd had her fill of the severe Detroit winters. Ben had also been very quick to say she should immediately open a new office in Santa Fe. He wasn't advocating that she stay home and sit around in a big red bow! It would be difficult to start over, but certainly not impossible. And Ben would be there, cheering her on in her new endeavor. She wouldn't be alone.

Chapel's stomach did a funny flip-flop, and she realized she wasn't doing too well physically with her ongoing elevator ride. Her hamburger and french fries were definitely uneasy over the roller coaster she was subjecting them to. She had to get out of there before she turned green. But go where? She was not ready to return to the apartment, and her purple feet and lack of a coat limited her choices, but she was getting seasick!

She figured out where to go, then concentrated

once again on the situation at hand. If she and Ben even considered getting married, the problem of where they would live had to be faced. He had done that in a manner he sincerely thought was appropriate. She had been the one to flip out, fly into a rage, and exit stage left, instead of right. It was a wonder she hadn't tossed in an ultramature "So there!" for good measure.

She hadn't handled that very well, she thought as she left the elevator and headed down the hall. She had to be honest with herself. The underlying message in Ben's actions was total commitment to him, their love. The anger she'd exploded with had been a shield against her fear. The fear of loving Ben Simmons.

"Oh, what have I done?" she said, throwing up her hands. "And what am I going to do now?" A sob escaped from her lips. "Chapel Barclay, if you cry, I'll never speak to you again!"

Ben was pacing the floor of Chapel's living room. Seventeen minutes, he thought. Chapel had been out in the hall for seventeen minutes! It was drafty out there, and weirdos could be wandering around. Enough was enough. This wasn't funny anymore, not one damn bit. He was going to haul her back in here and— Wrong. He was going to very quietly request that she return to the safety and warmth of the apartment. Then they would sit down and calmly discuss the matter. Maybe she'd like a cup of hot chocolate with a marshmallow on top. But first he had to convince her to come back inside.

He strode to the door, took a deep breath, then carefully opened it.

"Chapel, I— Chapel? Dammit, where is she?"

Ben hurried to the next apartment and pounded on the door. It was opened by a surly-looking man holding a beer can.

"Yeah?" the man said.

"Have you seen a young woman with cinnamon-colored hair and purple feet?" Ben asked.

The door was slammed in his face.

"Dammit to hell!" he muttered, heading for the elevator, his mind racing. Where was Chapel? Where in the hell was she? She wouldn't leave the building without a coat, would she? He should have gone after her the minute she stormed out. But, oh, no, not hotshot Simmons. He'd sat there grinning like a fool waiting for her to make her embarrassed reentry. He was a louse! A real sleazeball. Nothing had gone right. Santa Fe in 1935. Cripes. Then he'd opened his stupid mouth and made that stupid, macho caveman remark. He had to find her!

Ben stopped the elevator on every floor, peered up and down the corridor, then hastily hit the next button. Nothing. There was no sign of Chapel, and a futile search of the lobby only added to Ben's worry and frustration. His last hope was the basement, and he hurried down the hall. The game room was empty. The area housing storage lockers was void of human life. The only place left was the laundry room.

And there he saw Chapel.

Her profile was toward him as she sat across the room slouched in a chair, staring at a spinning dryer. His heart thundered as he looked at her. Her hair tumbled over her shoulders in a silky cascade. Her sweater was molded to her full breasts, and her jeans hugged the gentle slopes of her hips, buttocks, and legs. On her feet were her goofy, wonderful, adorable purple slippers. She was Chapel, and he loved her. The icy fear he'd felt when he couldn't find her slowly dissipated and was replaced by his deep love for this woman.

He walked slowly forward and picked up a chair, placing it next to Chapel's in front of the dryer, and sitting down.

"Hi," he said quietly.

"Hello," she said, not looking at him.

"I've seen this movie," he said, gesturing toward the colorful clothes whirling around in the dryer. "Want me to tell you how it ends?"

"Mmm."

"Chapel, look, I . . . I'm really sorry about what I said. You know I don't believe a man has superior rank in a relationship. I just feel so strongly about Santa Fe, and I know we'd have a wonderful life there together. I handled the whole thing like an idiot, and—"

"No, you didn't," she interrupted, turning to face him, tears shimmering in her eyes. "You were so sweet up to the point that you got despicable. I overreacted and I'm the one who's sorry. I've been sitting here going over everything in my mind. Ben, I'm not saying I refuse to move to Santa Fe. What I can't agree to is the commitment that acceptance would mean. I can't do that part yet. Not yet."

The fear of loving him, Ben thought. It still held her in an iron grip. He had to conquer it, but he was running out of time! "I understand," he said, smiling at her gently. "Come on. It's chilly down here. Let's go home, Chapel."

He reached out his hand palm up, and she looked deep into his eyes for a long moment before cradling her small hand in his. He stood and drew her up against him, kissing her softly, tenderly, then gathering her close to his chest. He held her, savoring the feel of her lissome body nestled against his. The fact that they were standing in a laundry room being serenaded by a humming clothes dryer was unimportant. He didn't wish to move, to shatter the intimacy of the moment. Chapel was in his arms, safe, protected, and he didn't want to let her go.

"Ben," she said against his sweater, "will you promise me something?"

"The world, darlin'."

"Please don't ever mention my outstanding, furious exit that landed me out in the hall, okay?"

He chuckled, causing her head to bounce up and down on his chest. "You've got it. My lips are sealed."

She tilted her head back and smiled. So did he.

"I love you, Chapel Barclay," he said.

"And I . . . I love you."

"I'm going to make you an offer you can't refuse."

"Oh?"

"Yep. We'll go upstairs, I'll fix us hot chocolate with marshmallows, and then . . . and then . . ."

"Then?"

"I'll show you Santa Fe, New Mexico, in 1935!"

Their laughter danced through the air as Ben circled her shoulders with his arm and they left the room, heading home.

Nine

Chapel had caught a cold.

She sniffled, sneezed, and coughed her way through the following day at work, accepting tea, aspirin, and sympathy from Beth. She refrained from telling Beth of the jaunt to the chilly laundry room, but was silently berating herself for stomping out the wrong door during her tantrum. She felt lousy, and decided she was being punished for her behavior.

Unable to push Ben's proposal of marriage nor his desire for them to live in Santa Fe far from the front of her mind, Chapel waited until Beth had gone to lunch, then picked up the telephone. An hour later she had spoken with three large law firms in Santa

Fe. The senior partner of each had been more than interested in her and her impressive credentials, and guaranteed her an interview should she choose to come west. Ben was right, she realized. There was definitely room for another lawyer in New Mexico. She'd think about it all later, when she felt better.

"At least it's Friday," Beth said, in the late afternoon. "Stay down the whole weekend. Soup, tea, juices, dry toast, oh, and Ben, of course. You'll be as good as new."

"Mmm," Chapel said, then sneezed.

"Go home. I know it's only four o'clock, but you don't have any more appointments. Should I call Ben and have him pick you up?"

"Don't be silly. I'm perfectly capable of driving myself home. I've managed to have colds on my own for years, Beth. When I'm sick, I don't want to see or speak to another human being."

"Well, as I recall there's a handsome human being living in your apartment."

"I'll simply tell him to ignore me until I'm better. Oh, ugh, my bones ache. I'll see you Monday."

"Take good care of yourself. Now, remember, soup, tea—"

"Yes, yes. Good-bye."

The drive home seemed to take forever. Chapel's head was pounding, her nose was running like a faucet, and her throat hurt. It was with dragging steps that she made her way down the hall and into the apartment. She called to Ben, and frowned when there was no answer. In her fuzzy state of mind she felt a flash of irritation that he wasn't there to greet her, then decided in the next instant that she was relieved, as he came under the human being status she wished to avoid.

After dropping her briefcase and coat onto the sofa, she entered the bedroom, changed into her red flannel granny gown, and crawled into bed. A few minutes later, she was sound asleep.

Ben entered the apartment an hour later, juggling two bags of groceries and a portable typewriter. He deposited his bundles on the kitchen table, then put the food away. Whistling softly, he wandered into the living room, and stopped in his tracks when he saw Chapel's briefcase and coat on the sofa.

"Chapel?" he said. "Why . . . what . . ."

He hurried into the bedroom and stood next to the bed, raking his hand through his hair as he gazed down at a sleeping Chapel. Her cheeks were flushed, and her hands were nestled by her face like a child.

"She's sick," he said. It was all his fault. He should have gone after her the moment she'd stormed out of the apartment the night before. She'd sat in that damn laundry room, and now she was sick. Thank goodness he was here to take care of her. No one should be alone when they didn't feel well, especially not his Chapel!

Striding back to the kitchen, Ben prepared a tray containing a cup of tea, a bowl of chicken noodle soup, sliced peaches, and a napkin in the shape of a teddy bear. He set the tray on the nightstand, then sat down on the edge of the bed.

"Chapel?" he said, placing his hand on her cheek. "Chapel, wake up, okay?"

"What?" she said, slowly lifting her lashes. "Ben?"

"Yes, I'm here. You really feel rotten, huh? I made you something to eat."

"No, I'm not hungry," she said, then sneezed three times in a row.

"Just try it. You need to keep your strength up. Sit up against the pillows."

"No!"

"Yes!" He propped the extra pillow behind her and lifted her upward.

"Oh-h-h, my head. I don't want to move, let alone eat. Ben, please just go away, and leave me be."

"No way. It's my fault you're sick, and I'm going to take care of you." He set the tray across her legs. "Sip a little tea."

"You don't understand. When I'm like this I don't want—"

"Drink," he said firmly.

"Leave me alone!" she said, tears spilling over onto her cheeks. "I don't want you here! I don't need you here!"

He stared at her for a long moment, then his jaw tightened and he got to his feet.

"I see," he said quietly. "I'll get out of your way then. I got the 'Dear Ben' mail from Santa Fe today, so I'll start on that. Call me if you need anything. I'll be in the kitchen." He turned and walked from the room.

"Oh, Ben," Chapel whispered, "I'm sorry. I didn't mean to be so hateful. I . . . oh, dammit!"

Ben sat slouched in a kitchen chair and ran his hand down his face as he drew a shuddering breath. Chapel's words screamed in his mind. "I don't want you here! I don't need you here!" Her voice had had a frantic edge to it, as though she felt threatened by his presence. Lord, those words had hurt. If she didn't want or need him near her when she was weak and sick, how could he ever hope she'd turn to him when she was in complete control? Her fear of loving him seemed to be growing, consuming her. She wouldn't even allow him close to her when she was ill.

"Oh, Chapel," he said, "I'm losing the battle. I'm losing you."

A crushing depression settled over him as he sat motionless in the silent room. He replayed in his mind every moment he had shared with Chapel from the first time he had seen her on the set of *Opposite Views*. He saw her smile, heard her laughter, could actually smell her special feminine aroma. His thoughts skittered to their lovemaking, and heat shot across his loins at the exquisite memories of what they had shared as they'd become one.

Dear God, how he loved her.

Had he been kidding himself from the beginning? He had been so positive that with time, patience, and the added ingredient of romance he would win Chapel. Romance. A helluva lot of good it had done him. Dear Ben was a washout. Chapel seemed to enjoy his romantic gestures, then in the next instant retreated behind her protective walls. He'd been so damn cocky and sure of himself, and everything had fallen apart. Statements like "I don't want you here. I don't need you here." spelled it out very clearly, and hurt like hell.

He wished he could chalk up Chapel's cutting words to the fact that she didn't feel well, but he couldn't. If she was going to accept her feelings of love for him, she'd want him with her now. It was like when his cat had died. He'd been miserable, and would have welcomed the loving sympathy and concern of a special someone. But Chapel didn't need him, not at all, not for anything.

With a deep sigh Ben pushed himself to his feet and went into the living room, where he plugged in the tree lights. Shoving his hands into his pockets he stared at the beautiful tree, then shifted his gaze to the fuzzy pink-and-white bear.

"What are you smiling about?" he said gruffly. "It's not kind to grin at a man who's been blitzed."

He walked to the bedroom door and leaned his shoulder against the jamb. The glow from the tree cast just enough light to make it possible for him to see Chapel sleeping in the bed. The tray was back on the nightstand, and he crossed the room and picked it up. The fact that none of the food had been touched did nothing to improve his gloomy mood. He returned the tray to the kitchen, then roamed restlessly around the living room. The evening ahead loomed like a series of bleak, empty hours, where he would have no choice but to face the hopelessness of his relationship with Chapel. Again her words hammered in his mind, and a painful knot tightened in his stomach.

The room seemed to close in around him, mocking him with its silence, declaring him an intruder, someone who was neither wanted nor needed there. Sweat dotted his brow, and the pounding of his own heart echoed in his ears. Spinning around, Ben yanked his coat out of the closet, unplugged the tree, and left the apartment.

* * *

Chapel stirred, then opened her eyes, blinking several times in the darkness. The clock on the nightstand stated it was just before midnight. Ben must have camped out on the sofa, she decided, so as not to disturb her. She'd been so rude, actually cruel to him, when he'd brought her the lovely tray of food. He'd even made her a teddy bear out of a paper napkin. She'd wake him up and apologize for her behavior. There was no excuse for the way she'd treated him.

She turned on the light, swung her feet to the floor, and pushed them into her purple slippers. Her headache was gone, and she felt much better. She'd tell Ben she was terribly sorry, eat whatever he placed in front of her, and urge him to return to the comfort and warmth of their bed.

Their bed, she mused. Yes, it was. And their lives, together. Their love. Their apartment, Christmas tree, teddy bear. She was half of a whole, woman for her man. Wife for a husband? Oh, yes! Yes! That's exactly whom she wanted to be, Benjamin Simmon's wife. When had it happened, the love defeating the insidious fear? It didn't matter when. What was important was that she was free at last to love her Ben. Nothing frightened her, because Ben would be at her side. She would move to Santa Fe with him, and they'd see the flowers in the spring. Together.

"Ben," she said, hurrying into the living room. "Ben, I— Ben? Oh, God, no! He's not here!"

She ran into the kitchen, then back to stare at the empty sofa. Where was he? It was midnight, and so terribly cold outside. Where had he gone? If only she could turn back the clock and erase the words she had said to him.

"I don't want you here," she said, her voice trembling. "I don't need you here. Oh, Ben, I didn't mean it. I'm sorry, so sorry."

She sat down on the sofa, pulled her legs up, then wrapped her arms around them and rested her chin on her knees. Ben's image danced before her eyes, so real, so alive, she felt as though she could reach out and touch him. But she couldn't, because he wasn't there. And it was all her fault.

Ben had given her so much, brought such joy to her life, and what had she given him in return? Nothing, except temper tantrums, her doubts, fears, insecurities. She'd even wanted his column banned, for Pete's sake. *She* was despicable!

For the next hour she sat on the sofa, listening intently for the sound of Ben's key in the lock. Fatigue began to numb her senses, and she realized she was chilled to the bone. With a defeated sigh, she shuffled back into the bedroom and slid between the blankets on the bed. Unable to keep her eyes open, she drifted off into a restless slumber.

She woke at eight the next morning and immediately thought of Ben. She dashed from the bedroom and gasped in dismay upon discovering he was not in the apartment. She felt achy and tired, but refused to return to bed. After showering, she dressed in jeans and a sweater, consumed two cups of tea, two aspirins, and a glass of orange juice. Just as she finished cleaning the kitchen she heard Ben's key in the lock.

She entered the living room as he came through

the door and closed it behind him. Her breath caught in her throat when she saw him, and she forced herself not to run into his arms. Lines of fatigue etched his face, and a stubble of beard was on his chin. His hair was in tumbled disarray, as though he'd repeatedly raked his fingers through it. He tossed his coat onto a chair and turned to look at her.

"Hello, Chapel," he said quietly, his voice sounding weary. "I see you're up. You must be feeling better."

"Yes, I'm much improved. Ben, I want to talk to you, tell you—"

"Not now," he interrupted, walking to the sofa and sitting down. "I'm beat. I'm also half drunk, I think. We'll talk later, for all the good it will do."

"What do you mean?" she asked, crossing the room to stand in front of him.

"I know when I'm licked. I fought hard for you, your love, our future together. Maybe I didn't always fight fair, but I did give it my best shot. But I lost. I was so damn sure I could show you that you had nothing to fear by loving me. I didn't intend to rob you of your identity, who you are. I wanted to add to your life. Every time I made some progress, saw you light up with one of those sunshine smiles, something would happen and I'd slide backward again."

"Ben, no!"

"I can't do it anymore, Chapel. I love you so damn much, but I'm fighting a losing battle. You said it yourself. You don't want or need me here in your life, with you. I have to face the facts as they are. I'm Dear Ben, and you never did like him a helluva lot. I'm leaving," he said, getting to his feet. "I'm going back to Santa Fe where I belong."

"Ben, please! Listen to me!"

"And hear what? That you love me, but that I'm on trial while you decide whether or not to chuck that love out the window? I can't live this way, not knowing from one minute to the next how you're going to perceive what I do or say. It's no good, Chapel. It just isn't going to work for us."

He brushed past her and went into the bedroom. Chapel sank onto the sofa as her trembling legs refused to hold her.

No! her mind screamed. No, Ben, please don't go! She had to talk to him. But what could she say that he would believe? Everything he had stated about their relationship was true. She had stood in judgment of him, accepted his romantic gestures one minute, questioned his motives for them the next. And worst of all, she had continually threatened to end what they had, should it prove not to her liking, adaptable to her life style.

The pain she had seen in the depths of his dark eyes had been of her making. She had hurt the only man she had ever loved. He wanted nothing now but to leave her as quickly as possible, return to Santa Fe, and get on with his life. She wanted him to stay, to believe her when she said she'd conquered the fear of loving him, that she wanted to be his wife, be with him, forever.

She wanted? Chapel thought, a near-hysterical sob escaping from her lips. What gave her the right to make further demands? She felt like a spoiled child who'd had her own way, but still whined for more. Oh, why had she weighed and measured Ben's actions? Why couldn't she have just loved him as he loved her? Oh, Ben!

Ben came back into the living room with his suitcase and set it on the floor. After retrieving his typewriter from the kitchen, he shrugged into his coat, then with slow steps, walked to the Christmas tree and plugged in the lights. His gaze lingered on the tree, as if he wanted to remember it forever, then he looked at the teddy bear.

"Chapel," he said, still looking at the bear, "I love you. I'll probably always love you. I'm sorry if I tried to force you into accepting a world that you really didn't want any part of."

Tears spilled onto her cheeks.

"I guess," he continued, "that romance doesn't always hold the answers after all. You taught me a lot about communication, though, about sharing, and I thank you for that. I never really understood what it meant before, nor realized how important it was. I just want you to know that—" he swallowed heavily as emotion choked off his words—"that you're really something."

He turned and picked up his belongings. At the door he hesitated, his back to Chapel, and then he left, closing the door behind him.

Ben was gone.

With a sob that was nearly a scream, Chapel called his name and ran to the door, leaning her head against it and sobbing uncontrollably. With tears blurring her vision she stumbled backward, then spun around to look at the tree. On impulse, she snatched up the bear and hugged it, buried her face in its fuzzy head, and wept. She sank to the floor and cried until she could cry no more. When exhaustion claimed her and she slept, she lay in the glow of the rainbow lights of the tree, her head resting on the pink and white teddy bear.

The weekend was a seemingly endless stretch of hours for Chapel. Lonely, empty hours. Hours without Ben.

She wandered through the apartment constantly sniffling, partly from her cold, but mainly because her tears never seemed to stop completely. Ben's absence shouted at her in the empty rooms, and she missed him with a painful intensity. The sight of the paper flowers on the table, her pink toothbrush with no blue one beside it, the empty space in the closet, all set her off on loud crying jags. The fuzzy fur on top of the teddy bear's head was smashed flat from the many times she had buried her face and wept.

On Monday morning she stared at her reflection in the mirror and decided she had never looked so awful. Her nose was sore and red, her cheeks pale, and there were dark smudges under her eyes. She could at least pass off her appearance as effects of her cold as long as she didn't cry. She really had to stop crying! But, oh, dear heaven, she was miserable. She missed Benjamin Simmons!

"It's your own dumb fault," she said to her image in the mirror. "You and your independence. You're a dunderhead, Chapel Barclay!"

At the office she lasted all of five seconds before bursting into tears and relating her tale of woe to Beth. The secretary gasped her dismay, shoved a handful of tissues into Chapel's hand, and listened with sympathetic frowns and shakes of her head. Beth did not, however, have a miracle cure for the ache in Chapel's heart.

Chapel tried desperately to bury herself in her work and put in hours of preparation for the custody case that was rapidly approaching. Just when she felt confident she would dazzle the judge with her brilliance, the woman Chapel was representing phoned to say she and her husband had reconciled, and wasn't that the most romantic thing Chapel had ever heard? Chapel mumbled her congratulations, hung up the receiver, and burst into tears.

Time crept slowly by.

Beth urged her to spend Christmas with the children and grandchildren descending on Beth, but Chapel refused, saying she wouldn't be chipper company. She also turned down invitations from fellow attorneys to New Year's Eve parties.

Ben filled her dreams at night and stood as a shadowy figure by her side during the day. She saw his smile, his dark eyes, his hair, thick and sun-streaked and silky. She envisioned his perfectly proportioned body, and allowed desire to flare as she recalled the ecstasy of their union. Ben.

On New Year's Day, Chapel took the decorations off the now drooping Christmas tree and packed them away. The janitor hauled the tree out the door, then she vacuumed up the pine needles and put the furniture back into place. Except for the teddy bear and the paper flowers, there was no trace of Ben Simmons left. But he was there. In her heart, mind, and soul, he was there.

Late that afternoon the telephone rang.

"Chapel Barclay?" a man asked.

"Yes."

"My name is Joe McBride. I realize I'm being presumptuous, but I'm a desperate man."

"I don't understand. Who—"

"You can tell me to buzz off if you want to, but look, it's about Ben."

"Ben?" she said, sitting bolt upright. "Has something happened to him? Is he sick? Hurt?"

"No, nothing like that. I'm his agent in New York. I had a bunch of interviews, talk shows, the whole bit, lined up for Ben and he's canceled everything. I spoke with him this morning at his home in Santa Fe and he— Well, he says he's quitting. He's not going to write the 'Dear Ben' column anymore."

"What? Why?"

"He says he's leading people astray by telling them that romance is the ticket to happiness. He's really bummed out, and I thought perhaps it had something to do with his relationship with you."

"Oh, no," she whispered.

"Miss Barclay, Chapel, will you talk to Ben? He's throwing away his entire career. He's also selling himself short. His column has turned things around for a great many people. I'm very worried about him. Maybe you have no feelings for him, I don't know, but I had to ask."

Various emotions swept through Chapel so quickly, her head was buzzing. She was awash with guilt, a sense of helplessness, then riproaring anger!

"He's being despicable again!" she exclaimed. "How dare he denounce romance after convincing me it's wonderful! Mr. McBride, I love Ben Simmons with every breath in my body. Teddy bears, Christmas trees, candlelight, didn't lead me astray; they helped lead me to love. He deserves a swift kick in the pants for the way he's behaving. Dear Ben has a responsibility to the couples in this country, by gum, and I have every intention of informing him of that fact!"

"Hot damn!" Joe said. "Go for it. Give him hell, Chapel!"

"I certainly will. Good-bye, Mr. McBride."

"Bye, sweetheart. I love ya!"

Chapel replaced the receiver and blinked once slowly as if coming out of a trance. Oh, good grief, what had she done? She'd actually told that Mr. McBride person that she was going to march herself to Santa Fe and tell Ben Simmons to shape up. She couldn't do that! But she had to! It was her fault that Ben had changed his mind about romance, was throwing away his career.

"Simmons," she said, "I'm on my way!"

Ben sat down behind his desk in the newsroom and sighed wearily. He'd just had another go round with Cappy, but he had stood firm. He was giving notice that he no longer intended to write the Dear Ben column. Cappy had finally thrown up his hands and agreed to call the owner of the paper, Austin's husband, Patrick Moran, and tell him of Ben's decision. The legal department would deal with whatever ramifications came from the irate editors involved in the syndicated column.

He just couldn't do it any more, Ben thought dis-

mally. He couldn't write a daily column urging people
to bring romance into their lives. Romance had gotten him a broken heart, and brought tears to the
beautiful green eyes of the woman he loved. Lord,
how he missed Chapel, ached for her. The days and
nights since he'd returned to Santa Fe had been a living hell. His heart was filled with love for her, while
his mind was ridden with guilt for what he had done
to her.

Her life had been in order until he'd charged into it
with his damn romantic candles, Christmas trees,
and teddy bears. Romance, his love, had brought her
no joy, only confusion, inner turmoil, and tears. He,
Benjamin Simmons, was despicable!

A sudden buzz of voices in the room brought Ben
from his reverie, and he glanced up absently. His eyes
widened as he saw what was causing the commotion.

Balloons! Dozens and dozens of helium-filled balloons, the strings held by a parade of young men in
khaki delivery-service uniforms, were being walked
into the newsroom.

"Ben Simmons!" the lead man boomed. "Delivery
for Mr. Ben Simmons!"

"Oh, good Lord," Ben said, slouching in his chair
with the hope of becoming invisible.

"Over there!" someone said, pointing at Ben.

"Mr. Simmons?" the messenger said. "Where
would you like your balloons, sir?"

"Don't tempt me to tell you where to put them," he
said, frowning. "Whose whacko idea was this?"

"The card, sir," he said, producing a small white
envelope. "Um, the balloons?"

"Tie 'em to something, I don't care," Ben said,

opening the envelope and pulling out a gold-edged card. It read *Teddy bears and balloons. Such a romantic combination.* "Chapel?" he said, jumping to his feet. "There's no name, but it's got to be. Hey, kid, did you see who ordered these?"

"That information is confidential, sir," the youth said. "Have a nice day."

"Chapel?" Ben repeated, staring at the card.

"Simmons," someone yelled, "get this garbage out of here. I've got an article to write!"

"What?" Ben said, looking up. "Oh, geez."

The messengers had made the rounds of the newsroom, tying the balloons to anything and everything available. The multicolored balls bobbed in the air as if dancing a jig. Some of the reporters were grinning, while others were none too happy.

"Take them home with you," Ben called out. "Don't you recognize something romantic when you see it, you dimwits?" Was Chapel in Santa Fe? he wondered. What exactly was she trying to say with the balloons?

A call to Chapel's office in Detroit produced Beth's voice on the machine. No one answered at Chapel's apartment. Ben was a nervous wreck. She *was* in Santa Fe, he just knew it, but he didn't know how to find her! All he could do was wait.

Two hours later Ben went to lunch. He'd snatched up the telephone every time it rang, had a sore neck from jerking his head around whenever the newsroom door was opened, and decided he needed a stiff drink with whatever he ate. He'd been waiting, watching, hoping, praying, for the sight or sound of

Chapel, but all he had to show for his nerve wracking morning was a zillion balloons!

Ben hardly tasted his lunch as the vision of Chapel Barclay stayed front and center in his mind. He wanted, dear God, *needed* to believe Chapel was really here in Santa Fe, that the balloons and reference to the teddy bear meant she loved him, was willing to accept him and his love in return.

He walked slowly back to the office, pushed open the door to the newsroom, then stopped dead in his tracks.

"Holy . . . cow," he whispered.

"Damn you, Simmons," someone shouted. "What's next? A herd of elephants? It looks like a damn funeral parlor in here!"

The balloons had company. Flowers of every variety, color, and fragrance, in pots, bowls, and vases, filled every nook and cranny of the room.

"Who has the card?" Ben asked. "Where's the card? I need that card!"

"Here," a man said, slapping it against Ben's chest. "Achoo! I'm allergic to this junk!"

Ben tore open the card and let out a whoop of pure joy. It read *Here's to you, to us, to Christmas trees, and flowers in the spring.*

"Achoo!" the man sneezed again. "I'm suing you, Dear Ben."

"Oh, geez," Ben said, snapping out of his state of euphoria.

"Mr. Ben Simmons!" a voice said.

"Dear Lord, now what?" Ben muttered, spinning around.

"Special delivery, sir."

Ben flipped open the envelope and felt the color drain from his face. "Oh, no," he said, shaking his head. "She wouldn't, would she? I'll wring her neck! Oh, man, what if she actually— Everybody out of this room!" he bellowed. "Clear the decks! Hit the road! Go!"

Nobody moved.

A man walked up behind Ben and peered over his shoulder at the paper.

"Hey, now," the reporter said, "it's going to get interesting. Dear Ben has a receipt here for two yards of three-inch red satin ribbon. I'd say the balloon and flower gal is showing up in a big red bow!"

"Fire!" Ben yelled. "Evacuate the building!"

Nobody moved.

"Dammit to hell!" Ben said, raking his hand through his hair.

"Hello, Ben," a soft voice said.

He nearly fell over his feet turning in the direction of the voice.

"Chapel!" he said, his gaze sweeping quickly over her.

She was clad in a trenchcoat, and was holding it shut with both hands. It came to her knees and revealed bare calves and feet. She was also wearing a smile.

"Chapel, I . . ." Ben started.

"Ben, I love you," she said, interrupting him. "I love you, and Santa Fe, and the babies we could have together. I love Christmas trees, teddy bears, balloons, and napkin flowers, as well as the real ones. I love who I've become since you touched my life with your whimsical, wonderful romance. I want you, I need you. Forever."

"All right!" someone said, and a cheer went up from the audience.

Ben strode to Chapel and scooped her up in his arms. "Hang on to that coat," he said, striding across the room and knocking over two pots of flowers on his way. "Do not take your hands off that coat!"

Chapel laughed and buried her face in his shoulder, remembering to hold the coat tightly closed. Ben walked down the hall to the accompaniment of echoing hoots and hollers from the congregation in the newsroom. He entered a reception room, kicked the door shut with his foot, and sank onto the sofa with Chapel on his lap.

"I love you," he said. "You're crazy, but I love you. You are really something. Oh, Chapel, I've missed you so much."

"And I missed you. Ben, I'm so sorry for the way I acted. I was terribly unfair to you and . . . please forgive me. I was frightened, scared to death of loving you. I didn't understand any of it, and I had everything twisted around. I realize now that I won't lose my identity by loving you. I'll gain your love, and that is the most precious gift I've ever had."

"Oh, darlin'," he said, and claimed her mouth with his.

The kiss was long and sensuous, and they were both trembling when Ben lifted his head.

"Will you marry me?" he asked, his voice husky. "Will you be my partner, my best friend, the other half of me? Will you walk with me through the flowers for the remainder of our springs?"

"Oh, yes," she said, tears clinging to her lashes.

"Thank you," he said softly, his eyes, too, unusually bright.

"Darling, please don't give up writing the column. 'Dear Ben' is important, he's needed."

"Yeah, you're right. There can never be too much romance in this world, or communication and sharing. I'll go on trying to convince people of that. We'll test out everything before it goes in the column. But, Chapel, about that coat . . ."

"Yes?" she said, eyebrows raised in innocence as she clutched it securely closed.

"You really have more on underneath it than just a big red bow, don't you?"

"Well, Dear Ben," she said, flicking her tongue over his lips, "why don't you carry me out of here, take me to a very private place, and find out for yourself?"

And he did.

THE EDITOR'S CORNER

Do you grumble as much as I do about there being too few hours in the day? Time. There just never seems to be enough of it! That seemed especially to be the case a few weeks ago when we were sitting here facing a scheduling board with every slot filled for months and months . . . and an embarrassment of goodies (finished LOVESWEPT manuscripts, of course). But, then, suddenly, it occurred to us that the real world limitations of days and months didn't necessarily apply to a publishing schedule. Voilà! 1986 got rearranged a bit as we created a thirteenth month in the year for a unique LOVESWEPT publishing event. Our thirteenth month features three special romances going on sale October 15, 1986.

What's so remarkable that it warrants the creation of a month? Another "first" in series romance from LOVESWEPT: A trio of love stories by three of your favorite LOVESWEPT authors—Fayrene Preston, Kay Hooper, and Iris Johansen. **THE SHAMROCK TRINITY!** Fayrene, Kay, and Iris together "founded" the Delaney dynasty—its historical roots, principal members, settings, and present day heirs. (Those heirs are three of the most exciting men you'd ever want to meet in the pages of romances—Burke, York, and Rafe.) Armed with genealogies, sketches of settings, research notes they'd made on a joint trip to Arizona in which the books were to be set, each author then went off alone to create her own book in her own special style. There are common secondary characters, running gags through the three books. They can be read in any order, stand alone if the other two books are not read. Each book features appearances by the heroes of the other two books, each is set during the same span of time—and yet, no one gives away the end of the other books. This is a fascinating trinity of stories, indeed, very clever and well-crafted, and packing all the wallop you expect in a love story by Fayrene or Kay or Iris.

Don't miss these extraordinary love stories. Ask your bookseller to be sure to save the three books of **THE SHAMROCK TRINITY** for you. They are:

RAFE, THE MAVERICK
LOVESWEPT #167
By Kay Hooper

(continued)

YORK, THE RENEGADE
LOVESWEPT #168
By Iris Johansen

BURKE, THE KINGPIN
LOVESWEPT #169
By Fayrene Preston

Now, as I said above, there is an embarrassment of goodies around here. And four excellent examples are your LOVESWEPT romances for next month.

Leading off is witty Billie Green with **GLORY BOUND,** LOVESWEPT #155. Gloria Wainwright had a secret . . . and Alan Spencer, a blind date arranged by her matchmaking father, was a certain threat to keeping that secret. He was just too darned attractive, too irresistible, and the only way to maintain her "other life" was for Glory to avoid him—in fact, to disappear from Alan's world. But he tracked down the elusive lady whose various disguises hadn't repelled him as Glory intended, but only further intrigued him. When Alan and Glory come face to face in her bedroom—under the wildest circumstances imaginable—firecrackers truly do go off between these two. This romance is another sheer delight from Billie Green.

After a long absence from our list, the versatile Marie Michael is back with **NO WAY TO TREAT A LOVER,** LOVESWEPT #156. This is the fastpaced, exciting—often poignant—love story of beautiful Charley (short for Charlotte) Tremayne and the deliciously compelling Reese McDaniel. After a madly passionate affair, Charley had disappeared to follow a dangerous life of intrigue. Now, she and Reese are thrown together again on the stage of a musical bound for Broadway. Charley tries to stay away from Reese—for his safety!—but cannot resist him! You'll want to give both of these endearing people a standing ovation as they overcome Charley's fears . . . and a few other stumbling blocks fate throws in their way.

Peggy Webb's **DUPLICITY,** LOVESWEPT #157, is a delightfully humorous book that also will tug at your heartstrings. Dr. Ellen Stanford knows it is reckless to bring a perfect stranger home to pose as her fiance, but she just can't face another family reunion alone. Besides, the myste-

(continued)

rious Dirk is about as perfect as a man can get—as good looking as Tom Selleck, masterful yet tender, and one fabulous kisser! But Ellen is dedicated to her work, teaching sign language to a gorilla named Gigi, and Dirk is pledged to a way of life filled with dangerous secrets. How Dirk and Ellen work through their various deceptions will delight you and no doubt make you laugh out loud—especially when Gigi gets in the act as matchmaker!

Rounding out the month is another fabulous romance from Barbara Boswell! **ALWAYS AMBER,** LOVESWEPT #158, is a sequel to **SENSUOUS PERCEPTION,** LOVESWEPT #78. Remember Ashlee and Amber? They were the twins who were adopted in infancy by different families. In **SENSUOUS PERCEPTION,** Ashlee located her sister— and fell in love with Amber's brother. Now it's Amber's turn for romance. She has finally broken out of her shell and left the family banking business. The last person she expects to meet, much less be wildly attracted to, is Jared Stone, president of a bank that is her family's biggest rival. Amber doesn't quite trust Jared's intentions toward her, but can't deny her overwhelming need for him. You'll cheer Jared on as he passionately, relentlessly pursues Amber, until he finally breaks through her last inhibitions. . . . A breathless, delicious love story!

At long—wonderful—last the much awaited **SUNSHINE AND SHADOW** by Sharon and Tom Curtis will be published. This fabulous novel will be on sale during the first week of September. Be sure to look for it.

Have a glorious month of reading pleasure!
Warm regards,

Sincerely,

Carolyn Nichols

Carolyn Nichols
  Editor
LOVESWEPT
Bantam Books, Inc.
666 Fifth Avenue
New York, NY 10103

LOVESWEPT

Love Stories you'll never forget by authors you'll always remember

 # LOVESWEPT

Love Stories you'll never forget by authors you'll always remember

☐	21760	**Donovan's Angel #143**	Peggy Webb	$2.50
☐	21761	**Wild Blue Yonder #144**	Millie Grey	$2.50
☐	21762	**All Is Fair . . . #145**	Linda Cajio	$2.50
☐	21763	**Journey's End #146**	Joan Elliott Pickart	$2.50
☐	21751	**Once In Love With Amy #147**	Nancy Holder	$2.50
☐	21749	**Always #148**	Iris Johansen	$2.50
☐	21765	**Time After Time #149**	Kay Hooper	$2.50
☐	21767	**Hot Tamales #150**	Sara Orwig	$2.50

Prices and availability subject to change without notice.

Buy them at your local bookstore or use this handy coupon for ordering:

Bantam Books, Inc., Dept. SW3, 414 East Golf Road, Des Plaines, Ill. 60016

Please send me the books I have checked above. I am enclosing $_____
(please add $1.50 to cover postage and handling). Send check or money order
—no cash or C.O.D.'s please.

Mr/Mrs/Miss_____

Address_____

City_____State/Zip_____

BANTAM
SHOP-AT-HOME
C·A·T·A·L·O·G

Special Offer
Buy a Bantam Book
for only 50¢.

Now you can have an up-to-date listing of Bantam's hundreds of titles plus take advantage of our unique and exciting bonus book offer. A special offer which gives you the opportunity to purchase a Bantam book for only 50¢. Here's how!

By ordering any five books at the regular price per order, you can also choose any other single book listed (up to a $4.95 value) for just 50¢. Some restrictions do apply, but for further details why not send for Bantam's listing of titles today!

Just send us your name and address and we will send you a catalog!